D.J. HAWKINS

This Mess You've Made

Editing by Olivia Paradice
Cover art by GermanCreative

This book was professionally typeset on Reedsy.
Find out more at reedsy.com

For those who had to leave

&

For those who chose to stay

*& for my mom, who has always been and will always be
my best friend, my rock, my inspiration*

Skin & Bones

Savannah

The mirror is the ultimate enemy.

It leaves you exposed under fluorescent lights, shame and restlessness reflected and leaving each and every one of us victims to our own faults. We entered this world judged and labeled, already martyrs for the common good. But we are the ones who continue to scrutinize our own actions and opinions.

The mirror is just a constant reminder of who we appear to be and who we will never become.

So, every feature is placed under a scalpel and resized or replaced. Permanent marker traces lines of precision and excises the assumed errors. Nothing will satisfy the bar that society has raised until our bodies are glorified mausoleums. We sacrifice our sanity, our innocence, for a sense of perfection that is merely a façade. We offer our souls in exchange for love: to be loved by someone else and to love ourselves.

The art of caving in has been perfected. Parts of us are always being chipped at or eroded away. We get chunks of our skin torn by bruised hands and fragments of our heart pierced by

1

double-edged words. We have become so good at falling apart and even better at failing to put the pieces back together.

But the mirror does not show me my flaws or my blessings. There is no feature I want to alter or keep. The image I see is neither beautiful nor ugly; exciting nor plain; familiar nor indefinite. The girl I see is simply a mask that has been there from the beginning and will remain until the end.

The reflection is the cover, the case. I am merely the stuffing. I am the marionette sewn from leftovers – stitched with shaky fingers, the tips tainted with juvenile dreams and misplaced ambitions. Every scar that ever spoiled my casing has been mended by my makers. Every time I made an error their quills dipped ravenously into various tints of toners and whiteouts, desperately trying to correct my irregular structure, my erratic disposition.

My makers have constantly fed me sugar-coated truths, hammered the doubts in me with fists of critique and promises of affection. They have forced a sense of acceptance onto me and I follow their guidelines because they are the only thing I know. So, I indulge in the safe confines of predetermined actions, adore the gaps in my recollections, and savor the sensation of free falling.

The penciled-on smiles and the patching of splintering wood are pointless. I am rotting beneath this skin, beneath the itchy outer covering that doesn't sit well in certain places. I could never fill this mold of theirs without peeling off an inner layer.

But I've learned to look through these puppet eyes, learned to stitch my own mouth shut when I see too much. Because I don't truly have a voice; I have no judgment, say, or value. There is a past that lies behind the mirrored girl, but it is intangible, inconsequential. My memories are blurred:

delicate undertones and washed-out images.

I know my place. I will always be covered up and stored away. I belong on a shelf, polished and proper. I am too defective - too scarred - to interact with other dolls.

I see all but my mouth is clinched shut.

* * *

"Please explain to me why we're up at the buttcrack of dawn again?" Abby's question greets me the same time her face does.

Jacklyn rolls her eyes and pushes her sister aside before pulling me into a quick embrace. "Let the girl open the damn door first, geez. Plus, 10 in the morning is hardly the 'buttcrack of dawn.' You just wake up in the afternoon on weekends."

Abby groans and shuffles into the house when I open the door wider. She immediately heads to the couch and drapes herself over the arm. "Still doesn't answer my question."

I close and lock the door before picking up an empty box near the foot of the stairs and extending it toward them. "This is why."

Jacklyn and Abby glance at each other with raised eyebrows. "A box?" Jacklyn presses the back of her hand to my forehead. "Are you feeling okay?"

I take two steps back and sigh. "I'm fine. My mom said she's enlisting our help to clear out my dad's office." I give Jacklyn the box. "So let's get going."

Abby scoffs, repositioning her body so she's laying across the entire couch. "Not that I don't mind a good dose of child labor, but why do we have to clean your dad's office? Why can't he do that?"

I pick up another box and hand it to her. "She said she'll pay the both of you. And my dad hasn't been here in months so there's no way it'll get done in time."

"In time for what?"

I start walking away from them, shoulders tensing. I move them up and down in an attempt to loosen the muscles.

"Sav?" I hear Abby's heels rapidly clicking against the hardwood, but still jump when she suddenly appears by my side. "In time for what?" She repeats, grabbing my arm to stop me from moving.

I lean against the wall and take a shuddering breath. "She wants to sell the house. Or they do. I don't know whose idea it was, but no one consulted me on the matter."

They take the box from me and wrap their arms around my frame, squeezing tightly for just one moment before releasing me again.

"Oh, Sav." Jacklyn runs a hand down my hair. "I'm so sorry, sweetie. It just came out of the blue?"

I sniffle, my nose and throat suddenly clogged. "At first she said they just wanted to remodel and declutter. But then this morning she called again and said they may be selling the house."

"No explanation or anything?"

"Unless…" Abby bites her lip and shares a look with Jacklyn. "Does this mean…?" She trails off when Jacklyn shakes her head. I have no idea what they're hinting at, but it seems like it'll only make me feel worse if I knew. "Never mind. That's beyond shitty that they didn't even talk to you."

I cover my face with shaking hands. "How is this fair? How could they do this to me? They're barely even here and leave me in this fucking shell of a house and I hate these white walls!" I throw the box at the wall but it makes a pathetic thump before landing perfectly on the ground. "But it's all I have."

"You have us. We've been friends for years and you won't get rid of us that easily." Jacklyn reaches out to me again, but I push them both away.

"That won't matter if I'm not here." I scrub my leaky eyes and wipe my nose on my shirt sleeve before collecting the box off the ground. "I guess there's no point in getting upset about it." My arms and legs feel heavy as I move into the office. "Not like I have a say in what happens to me anyway."

We're silent as we crowd into my dad's office and examine the scattered papers and dust lined shelves. Jacklyn opens the lone window but the air we breathe in remains stale.

Abby sets her box down and groans, "Your dad has so much junk! Didn't he ever throw anything away?"

"And when was the last time he cleaned this place? There is dust everywhere!" Jacklyn wipes a finger across the desk and then holds up a grey, dirt covered digit.

Abby's eyes narrow in on an open book on the desk. Her hand hovers over it before suddenly, she pushes it over the edge. Both Jacklyn and I just watch as she proceeds to wipe everything off the desk, her breath becoming ragged. "Since when do the kids have to clean up their parents' mess?" Then she turns to me, lips pressed together. "Let's pack up his shit and then get out of here."

The three of us work in silence for what feels like forever, stacking staplers on top of notebooks on top of books. I notice Jacklyn and Abby keep throwing each other looks that I can't even begin to decipher. But I guess it doesn't really matter.

My dad left months ago for reasons I was never told, but I'm not a child. I know he didn't want to be here. I just don't know the reason why. And even though he's been gone, there are still pieces of him everywhere. His favorite mug in the cupboard, his lucky pair of socks in the dresser, and the most noticeable: his 17 year-old daughter.

I'm packing up my box, filled to the brim with odds and ends my dad has accumulated over his time in this house, and am filled with a strange sense of emptiness. If I were to pack up all my belongings, the articles that actually mean something to me, how many boxes would they fill? Would anything of mine be packed away in someone else's box because I meant that much to them?

"Your dad sure held onto a lot of stuff. He has receipts from the early 2000s. So pointless." Jacklyn takes a handful of yellowing slips and places them in her box.

Abby, on the other hand, is inspecting an empty pill bottle. "These are sleeping pills. I guess you had to take them when you were younger?" She's asking me, but I don't remember taking anything to help me sleep. And I definitely don't need them now because I sleep more than I do anything else.

She digs into the file box on her lap and pulls out sheets of paper. After quickly scanning them, her eyes flick to mine. "Have you ever looked at your medical records, Sav? It seems like your dad kept quite a few."

I walk over to her and lean over her shoulder. There are so many words on the page, it makes my head hurt.

"What does it say?" I motion for her to read it out loud.

Abby clears her throat and snaps the paper tighter. "It seems like you started taking anxiety meds and antidepressants when you were... wow, only 8 years old."

"That's so young." Jacklyn whispers, perched on the edge of the desk.

"You were taking Duloxetine for generalized anxiety disorder and Fluoxe- Fluoxetine? I'm not sure how to pronounce either of these honestly. But this one was for major depressive disorder."

"It feels like 8 is too young to start taking all this medication, but I know that a lot of them can be taken once the kid is 7." Jacklyn shrugs, taking the paper from Abby. "What medication are you on now?"

"Uhm, I'm supposed to stop taking Buspirone soon and switch to Lexapro, I think. Not sure. My mom doesn't trust me with the medication so Bailey and her parents kind of handle all that when she's away."

Suddenly, Abby whips out a stack of photos. She flips through a few before stopping and tilting her head. "Hey, Sav. Who is this little boy?"

Both Jacklyn and I look over her shoulder to examine the photo. There is a little version of me, in a blue and white polka dot dress, curls tied up by ribbons. I am standing on the edge of a large, rippling lake and next to me is a little boy, who holds my hand in his. His dark, wavy hair is ruffled by the wind and he's covered in mud, but he's smiling like he just won a million dollars. His smile is so wide it hurts my own mouth and I take a step back.

"Must be a childhood friend," says Abby, waving the photo around. " Like, from before even we met you. How old are you in this picture? Like 5?"

"I guess this was also before the accident since you're near water. "

"I don't... I don't remember." I don't, but that boy's smile is all I can see now. Flashes erupt behind my eyelids, laughter echoing in my head but no clear images come to me.

"Oh hey, here's another picture. Isn't this the tulip you and your dad planted?"

I don't have to look at the picture to see what she sees. There is the tulip, a seed my dad gifted me and we planted together. There is my dad, looming behind me as I celebrate the flower's growth. And there is the little boy, whose name and memory refuses to come to me, with his hands in the dirt.

Jacklyn tries to hand me the photo but I shake my head. "Looks like he helped plant the tulip. I wonder where he is now."

I continue to shake my head, the flashes blinding me as I try to remember that day, those moments, this smiling child whose dirt-covered fingers clasp mine. But I can't, and the effort is causing a migraine.

"Okay," I let out a breath. "Let's just pack up these boxes and go somewhere else."

"Ugh, yes, let's go! I'm tired of inhaling dust fumes." Abby discards the photos and wipes off her hands before closing her box and sprinting out the door.

I grab the photos from the desk, hoping they will jog the memories I've lost. Or at least give me clues into a past I never knew I had.

Third Degree Burns

Aryn

Death is inevitable.

We are born just to die. And we all die. Some sooner than others, some far too late. But we all end up in the ground or stuffed in a vase.

There are those who burn like a candle. The flame may flicker but death comes at the very end, when there is no more wax to melt. It is slow, unquestionable, and expected. Candles, unless snuffed out, fade until there is nothing left.

There are those who burn out like a match. Quick to ignite and even quicker to go out. There's not even enough time to flicker. It is heart-wrenching and comes without warning. Matches burn brilliantly but are gone with the breath of a whisper.

And then there is me, and a million other people, who live with strong pulses and thick skin. Death is at the end of the tunnel but we are neither a candle nor a match. We do not fade or burn out. We implode.

We are born just to die and we are all born sick.

It's not an airborne disease that rides a puff of breath and sticks like tar along the lining of our lungs. Or a physical ailment that creates hairline fractures in our fragile bones until we're just a pile of flesh.

But we were born with this sense of hopelessness, trapped inside bodies of color and given names that shouldn't define us but do. We try our best to create ourselves with the leftovers: inherited dimples or lop-sided grins. We lose bits and pieces along the way, realizing that porcelain is stronger than flesh and deception mends broken hearts better than honesty. Any shred of dignity or trace of individuality is stomped out by the fear of rejection.

There is no room for mistakes, no mercy for the weak. One falter, one uncertainty, will crash the system. So we sacrifice and barter, losing any hope at reclaiming what was once ours. What could have been ours.

I broke the system. We all break it sooner or later. Bending a rule to fit our mood then scrambling at the last minute to lay it straight. We bruise our knuckles and chip our teeth. Shatter a heart and beat the mind.

I've tried to fix it but my fingers can't thread a needle to stitch the seams. The loose ends are frayed and the broken pieces are jagged. I've spilt blood and drained myself dry before realizing that damage control doesn't accept failure, doesn't believe in trial and error.

We go through life either terrified of death or making mistakes. The truth is, both are inescapable. But some deaths are more tragic and some mistakes should never be made. Some deaths are deemed necessary and some mistakes get swept under the rug.

When you experience the flickering of life secondhand like I have – a candle that was snuffed out before its time – you start to notice the signs of death. I don't mean diseases that destroy the mind and body. I can tell when someone is imploding.

The first sign: flowers don't grow where we're bent and broken.

The cracks never get fixed.

* * *

"Storms remind me of sex. Starts off weak and makes you jump. But it always ends in a bang!"

Corey is perched on my bed, an igloo of covers and pillows sheltering him from the disaster running loose on the streets. The shades are pulled down but flashes of lightning cast ominous images across the walls.

I resist the urge to press my knuckles into the soft flesh of his scalp. Just the thought makes the bones in each finger pulse and the skin peels from recent exposure. Tiny tears of red crystalize in the dry patches of calloused palm.

I clear my throat. "You get scared every time you have sex?"

The rain knocks nervously against the windows and lightning whispers sweet nothings across the dark sky. The thunder is actually a war cry and the sound rips holes into the grey clouds.

Corey's tongue pokes out from between his teeth. "Nooo. I just..." He fidgets beneath his temporary shelter. "It just takes some time to get the rhythm going."

"Well, if having sex with you is like a storm, then I definitely don't see the appeal."

"What? Why not? I bring the lightning and the thunder!" He leans toward the roaring outside. "A finale like that is impressive."

"I wouldn't be impressed if you made a mess everywhere. Or if you were loud and didn't actually deliver." I raise an eyebrow, glancing from him to the window. "Seems like the lighting and sound effects are compensation for something else."

He scoffs, face-planting into my bed and speaking into the mattress, "You're so insensitive. As my best friend, you shouldn't attack my most valuable possession."

I stifle a laugh. "Is there really anything valuable down there?"

The windowpane rattles as tree branches knock, begging for solace from the oncoming storm. Lightning kisses the moist earth and the smell of burnt spring leaves fills the room. The thunder beats rhythmically and seems to shake everything around us.

Corey lets out a groan, "We're going to die, Aryn. All 7 billion of us. The storm is going to get worse. I can feel it in my bones."

I tongue the chapped skin on my lips. I want to tell him that the world is already halfway there. Binging, purging, and everyone holding their breath because there's no air left to breathe.

But I swallow the words and jump on the bed beside him. "Well, we're still alive. Isn't that good enough for you?"

He looks up at me from beneath the onslaught of cotton and feathers. "I guess so. But for how long? If possible, I at least want to choose how I die."

His voice drowns out the rain. Increases in frequency until the window cracks. Unless you cut the cord that tethers you to this world, you have no choice in your death. The ability to choose is both a reprieve and a burden. I was never granted that choice.

Fire chose me years ago; tempted me with razor sharp flames and claimed my soul. I was a willing victim. A grateful sacrifice. I can already feel its claws inching up my thighs, curling around my wrists. I love the pain and deserve the burns.

"I would like to go peacefully in my sleep. Anything else is terrifying." Corey squints his eyes at me, wrapping the blanket around him until he resembles a burrito. "Eh, dying from too much sex would be pretty awesome, too." His voice quivers beneath his ever-present teasing.

I try to pat his back through the comforter. "Well, you have plenty of years left to accomplish death by sex. But first, don't you actually have to you know... have sex?"

He sticks his tongue out and then sneaks a hand from beneath the covers, blinding reaching for the remote. He clicks a few buttons before successfully turning on the TV. I get off the bed, not in the mood to watch re-runs from two-decades ago. I lift the shade and press my ear against the window, closing my eyes as the thunder purrs just for me.

What Corey doesn't understand is that death doesn't scare me. Not anymore. Fire cannot truly kill me. It owns me, yes. But I can't burn or be put out.

Then again, there is more than one way to die.

13

Outside Looking In

Savannah

There are quivering voices living rent free inside my head, whispers upon whispers coming from lips sewn shut – each mouth laced with colorful thread, hoping the silence will be warning enough.

But the silence covers everything so well and the world continues to spin upon her tilted axis, dancing in dizzying circles beneath the endless sky. Her children upchuck their dreams as she grants them nothing less and nothing more than twenty-three degrees.

Within these twenty-three degrees are coasts lined with chipped teeth and barbed wire meadows. I have seen tear-filled rivers and blood-soaked cities in my dreams – so vivid I can taste salt and smell iron. There are multi-colored thumbtacks to trace where I've been and empty spaces to show where I'll never end up.

It's like everyone can only go so far. We are permitted to travel left or right, can only move numbered steps when going forward or back. Everyone is born with a set destination: to be robbed of their voice and thrown into the fire, or to be in command and hold the match.

I've dragged my feet through flooded trenches, waiting for the fire to go out but drowning in the process. There is no salvation, no future. My days tick by slower and slower until time freezes altogether. I relive the nightmare – survive the massacre over and over again, never changing anything even though I know the outcome.

And even though I buckle myself down, the world continues to throw me against the wall. The clock strikes midnight and even I lay in the debris, dizzy and reeling.

I was born to feed the fire, after all.

* * *

"Do I look okay? Spinach teeth or pit stains?" Abby lifts her arms above her head and shakes her hips. Her tongue runs along movie-star bleached teeth as she throws a Cheshire cat grin my way.

As she does a 360, her floral print skirt balloons around her with prima ballerina grace. The abundant golden locks piled into a chaotic bun spring loose and cascade down her back in silky waves. She stares at me beneath half-lidded eyelids coated in a light shade of purple powder, eyelashes curled towards her eyebrows to reveal toffee eyes.

I pry my lips open. "You look gorgeous as always."

She throws another toothy grin my way before smacking her lips together and sliding into a cracked, plastic chair. Back erect, eyes smoky and downcast, chest protruded.

"I try, I try." She produces a tube of shimmering, pink lip gloss and slowly applies two coats to her already sparkling lips.

"This is my favorite, Sav. You really have to get some." She smacks her lips together. "Tastes like strawberries." Eyes turn and stare for a moment too long.

A white flash of envy spreads from my fingertips to my baby-blue toes. I gather an inch of skin between my nails, compelling the feeling away but it wraps itself around me.

These are the moments when I am filled with untamable sensations that sit heavy in my chest and suck the air from my lungs. They curl stiff, cold fingers around my throat and pull me six feet under. I've tried so many times to bleed them out, but they live in the darkest corners of me.

"I'm so glad the day is almost over. We're hanging out after school, right?"

I nod, turning my water bottle around and around so the water catapults against the plastic. "Jacklyn said we're going to Chipotle for dinner." Just the thought of food makes my throat burn. I unscrew the top to the water bottle and tip it back until I'm drinking in air. I look across the table, but Abby is already scouting the cafeteria.

She doesn't stay long: she is a wanderer, a social butterfly with a plethora of cocoons. She scoots out of the chair with dignity and purpose, walking steadfast to deliver the next punch line, to grace someone with her presence. She leaves behind a bubble of cold air and a sickly-sweet aroma of peach and cream, glitter corrupting the otherwise food-splattered table. I can't help but stare at the empty chair, questioning the space that is no longer occupied.

Vacant.

I look around the cafeteria, wondering why I'm always alone, why I allow myself over and over again to be okay with it. As I'm scanning the room, I notice a boy across the room, poking at the food on his tray. Alone. Just like me.

He is hunched over the table, which is tucked in the corner, and he seems solely focused on mashing his food to pieces. I trace the outline of him, wondering if I, too, resemble a dejected doll. If someone looks at me and thinks "lonely."

I try convincing myself to look away, but it's too late. He must've felt me staring because his head snaps up and we make awkward eye contact. He scans my surroundings, the empty table, the lack of friends, and then he looks me up and down, similar to the way I just examined him. When he finds what he was looking for, we just stare at each other. My pulse jumps as he starts to stand and I panic, reaching for my bag in case I need to flee.

But then a chair is pulled out next to me and arms lace around my neck. I swallow deeply, looking up into warm, coffee colored eyes. Jacklyn's cheeks are painted a soft pink, a smile wreaking havoc across her face. She releases me, placing a brown-bagged lunch and a leather-bound novel on the table.

"Whatcha looking at?" Her voice is light, almost musical. She takes a baby carrot out of the bag, chewing absent-mindedly as her eyes quickly trace the leather binding.

I shake my head, swallowing the panic. "Nothing. Nothing at all." But I sneak a peek over at the boy and breathe a sigh of relief when I realize that another boy has joined him. His attention is no longer on me and I can focus on something else now. Like Jacklyn.

"I saw Abigail leave. Where did she go?"

I start picking at my flaking nail polish and shrug. "Making her rounds."

"Yes, she does have a reputation to uphold." She giggles, bending the corner of a page back and forth.

17

I feel like I should speak, but my words are always lost in translation, bottled up in the silence. I can't really complain, though, because I enjoy the low hum that comes with no dialogue, no pretenses.

I begin melting into the chair, letting the cold air wash over me. But I see Jacklyn pull the book tight to her chest, the leather sticking to her skin as she tries to inhale its words, and I have to look away. I can feel Jacklyn's adoration for the story hidden behind ancient leather: her idolization of the carefully scripted verses and her obsession with any life other than her own.

While everyone wishes for a different life, a better life, I am the odd one out. I do not wish to be saved or to live vicariously through others. I just *am* and the one thing I wish for is to cease to be. The truth is, even if I wanted to immerse myself in fictional worlds, I would feel like an intruder who does not fit into that space.

This fact does not come as a surprise but rather a reaffirmation. I am the outsider looking in, the omnipresent third person narrator. This role fits me well and I indulge in being able to see behind closed doors. I enjoy being able to fill empty space with nothing more than my mere presence. That's all I have to be: there.

But again, that emptiness is filled with radiance and volume. Abby stands in front of us, her yellow ringlets lying perfectly over her shoulders.

I was waiting for the static, for a silence that fit snug and covered me completely. The void that would have offered me a temporary numb.

"Who were you trying to recruit now?" Jacklyn snickers, not looking up from the white-washed, crisp pages.

Abby snaps her gum and winks at me. "Some of the freshies. They said they were interested in trying out for the play or for lacrosse. But I'll convince them to join the softball team, just you wait."

Jacklyn sighs, placing her book face down. "Not everyone can be as dedicated as you, Abigail."

Abby purses her lips and the lip-gloss shimmers beneath the fluorescent light. She slides into the seat across from me, throwing a tight-lipped smirk in my direction before smoothing down her ruffled skirt and turning to Jacklyn. "Well, I'm the captain for a reason then, aren't I?"

Jacklyn shrugs, a baby carrot placed between her fingers like a cigarette. "I guess. Were you able to convince any of the seniors to fail and stay back a year?"

Abby opens a small compact mirror. "Still haven't accomplished that. All of you seniors just want to leave!"

"Well, the goal of high school is to leave after four years. No point in staying longer than necessary."

Abby pouts, letting her composure slip. "But the future's so scary. College is so scary! What if this is as good as it gets?"

I try to stay tuned to their voices, to their words. But all of it is so inconsequential. I can't find the strength to hold onto sentences full of clipped syllables and pointed index fingers.

I slip out of my chair, taking the time to push it in so it doesn't scrape against the floor. Jacklyn doesn't notice the deliberate action. Neither of them notice when I stand up and start walking away. At first, I think no one notices when I turn around, one inch from the outside, waiting for someone to call me back. But then I see him again and he's standing, like he's getting ready to sprint toward the door. I can't gauge the expression on his face, but I don't like it. I don't like him looking at me like he can see inside my head.

When the door softly clicks behind me, the hairs on my arms stand up. The urge to turn around tugs at my ankles but I already know it won't make a difference. I am alone even on the inside.

It's true: the world keeps spinning, everyone moving along with it. But I stand still.

Inferno

Aryn

I only dream of fire.

Every night when I close my eyes, the room is doused in gasoline and I am the one who holds the lighter. Every night when I close my eyes, I set myself ablaze.

I am used to the flames biting into my flesh and licking away the skin inch by inch. But I can never get used to the screaming. I never knew I could make such a desperate, guttural sound. I scream for hours, until my throat aches and my lungs are deflated.

The odor of my burning flesh stains everything: the bed-sheets, the floorboards, the poorly placed wallpaper. In the distance, I can hear voices screaming my name. I search the room for a familiar face but it is colored red and orange. The fire is so bright and I close my eyes in hope of escaping the hellish hues but even my eyelids are set on fire.

Eventually, my body is reduced to ash and that's all I am: black residue that stains the hardwood and seeps into the cracks. The flames die down and all is silent. And then, when

I think the nightmare is finally over, my mom walks in.

Tears mark inky trails down her creamy skin and her shoulders shake under her too big sweatshirt. She whispers my name over and over as she sweeps the fragments of me under the rug. She walks out the door, never looking back at the spot where I used to lay and she locks me in. Locks me away.

I wake up caked in sweat and out of breath. The sheets are coiled around my thighs, torso, and throat. I can still feel the flames grinding away at my bones. For a while, my mother would be standing next to me, woken by my screams. She would sit with me for hours until I fell back to sleep, wiping away my sweat with wet washcloths. It's become so commonplace in our house that she can just sleep through it now.

I dream of fire, but even when I'm awake it's hard to tell what's real when images of the past keep reoccurring in the present:

My father is being filled with oxygen because his lungs can't properly inflate. My sister lies under the scalpel for hours as her skin is clipped and sewn back together. My mother is energized by cheap coffee from a vending machine. She fights back tears for me; she remains calm for me. And I am curled into a plastic chair in the waiting room, fists beating the wall and wishing I could take it all back.

The best solution is to stay awake. I am still confronted by the past but my mind races to stay ahead of the memories. I trace the cracks in the ceiling, the tan paint curling into itself. I walk the parallel lines on the carpet until my legs give out. I look out the window and try to count how many fireflies hover in the night sky. But there are no tiny, blinking lights –

only darkness. The trees are merely silhouettes serving as the night's backdrop.

Sometimes, when the darkness refuses to leave, I am the one who sweeps the fragments of me under a rug, the million screaming pieces finally put to rest.

* * *

"Dude, let's go. I'm so fucking hungry." Corey walks up to me, his hands gripping his stomach. He leans his head against my locker. "I'm so hungry that your arm looks like sausage to me right now."

I chuckle, stuffing my hoodie into my bag and closing the green metallic locker. "I'm coming. I just need to hand in my history paper. Want to wait in the car?"

He shakes his head, "Nah, I'll tag along. It's too hot to wait in the car."

I shake the keys in my pockets. "Air conditioner."

"Too late, bro. I'm too lazy to turn around." Corey stops and dips a hand into his bag. He pulls out a Snickers, sniffs the wrapper and rips it open. A satisfied groan erupts in the back of his throat. "Why are you handing the paper in anyway? It's not due until May."

I shrug, grabbing the Snickers from him and stuffing the rest in my mouth. "I didn't do much over spring break."

He stares at me with a slack jaw. "Did you just... My Snickers-" I ignore him and walk into Ms. Jacob's room.

"Hello, Aryn. Just two more months! Excited?"

I pull a folder from my bag and place the paper I used as a distraction on her desk. "I am so ready. This year has been hell."

She nods, tapping her fingers against the desk. "I had no problem giving you an extension, if you needed one."

Ms. Jacob, a 25-year-old grad student, is the TA for my AP U.S. History class. She is by far my favorite teacher, but she is often so caring that it becomes intrusive. The thing I like most about her is her tolerance for silence. She will listen if you need to talk, talk if you need a distraction, or simply sit with you if you are feeling particularly alone.

But at this moment, I don't need any of those things.

I shake my head and feel the muscles in my mouth twitch. "Thank you but I really just wanted to get it over with." There is a pause and I see her take a deep breath. "It was an interesting prompt to write about anyway! I have to go, Corey's waiting for me. I'll see you tomorrow, Ms. Jacob!"

She stands up, a frown firmly set in place. She doesn't say anything, though. She knows I won't wait around to listen.

So I walk out on her, her palms splayed across the desk, and speed walk my way back down the hallway toward Corey. I just grab him by his forearm and start pulling him along with me.

"Dude," Corey complains but matches my pace, tripping over his shoelaces in the process.

When we reach my car, I quickly slide into the driver's seat and place my head against the steering wheel. It takes me a moment to catch my breath.

Corey turns to me with red cheeks and watery eyes. "I'm too fluffy for extended exercise. You know this and yet you still torture me." He points to dashboard and fans himself. "Air please."

I oblige, inhale a burst of cold air, and pull out of the school parking lot. "When will all the teachers stop looking at me like

I'm some sad orphan who needs to be coddled? I'm tired of everyone walking on eggshells around me."

Corey browses through the radio stations, nodding his head to various beats as they flit by. "I can't say I understand the feeling, but they're just trying to show they care. It is almost the anniversary and –"

"Yeah, I don't need to be reminded."

"Dude, don't get bitchy with me. All I'm saying is that this could be a difficult time for some people so they're trying to be understanding. Even if they don't actually understand what you're going through. Okay?"

I roll my eyes as the air quickly pumps from the vents and covers my entire body in a thin coat of ice. My muscles loosen and I lean back into the seat.

Ms. Jacob means well but I won't talk to her. She will just try psychoanalyzing me and when she realizes that there is no simple solution, she will send me to the school therapist.

I already been to a therapist. Diagnosis: angry. There were other words thrown around like *self-destructive* and *unstable*. But I don't feel self-destructive or unstable.

I don't even feel angry most of the time. I feel spent, empty, like a hollowed out acorn that's been left to be stepped on. And then I am terrified, shaken to the core. The past never fails to sneak up on me and send me sprawling to my knees. I can never anticipate when the memories will seize me or whether they will soothe or intensify the pain.

I lower the volume and turn to Corey when we hit a stop sign. "Where to?"

Corey grins, putting his feet up on my dash. "Your mood shifts never cease to amaze me. If you're done being a brat, how about some Taco Bell?"

"You act like I'm your younger brother or something." I raise an eyebrow.

He shrugs, waving a hand in my direction. "You may be older, but everyone knows I'm wiser." He pouts and rubs his stomach. "Now feed me."

I turn left, heading down the boulevard. "I'm going, I'm going."

Corey leans back further in the passenger seat and pats his stomach. "Such a good little brother."

I turn the music back up, wanting to tune out his voice as he rants about the forbidden marriage of cheddar cheese and hot sauce. But then it becomes obvious he wants attention, because he changes the subject.

"So that girl. What's going on there?"

I roll my eyes, "What girl?"

"The girl you were having a staring contest with in the cafeteria today!"

Sighing, I turn the music off. "I don't know. I was waiting for you to show up, since you're always late." I give him a pointed look. "I was just sitting there and then it felt like someone was staring at me and it was her. So, I stared back." I shrug, not seeing the big deal.

"It's rude falling in love while I'm not around." Corey sucks his teeth.

"Ha. That's not what happened. If anything, it was a creepy encounter. Plus," I turn my blinker on and turn into Taco Bell's drive-thru. "She was clear across the room, so maybe she wasn't even looking at me. I could barely tell what she looked like!"

Corey hums in agreement as he begins rattling off what he wants to order. I, on the other hand, try to think of the staring contest in the cafeteria as merely a chance encounter. Because what I felt when the girl and I made eye contact proved it was something more. But I can't name what it was, and that's the scary part.

Red Light, Green Light

Savannah

"Whoa, bitch. Your tan is ridiculous." Abby sticks her head out the car window and whistles, motioning to Bailey's darkened skin.

Bailey blushes as she slides into the backseat. "That's what happens when you're in Miami for two weeks. I'm just surprised I didn't get a sunburn." She pouts, poking her arms and thighs cautiously. "At least I don't look like a vampire anymore. That means no more Twilight jokes!"

Abby shrugs in the passenger seat, switching radio stations every few seconds. "Yeah, yeah. But you still look like Bella Swan so…"

Jacklyn giggles from the driver's seat, looks over her shoulder, and pulls away from the curb. The breeze slips in through all four windows and whips my hair against my face. I shift in my seat, grimacing at the accumulating sweat, and turn to Bailey.

She stares at me, cheeks still slightly flushed. A smile slowly envelopes her face and she leans in. "Hi," She whispers, kissing my cheek. Her arms form a circle around me, her strawberry scent strong even amidst the wind. "I missed you, Sav. Two weeks felt like an eternity."

My heart hammers inside my chest and I take a deep breath. I dig my fingers into her back, staring out the window at the blurring scenery. My throat tightens: I want her to let go but I feel cold without her touch. I close my eyes, fighting the acid in my throat.

"An eternity in hell. What did we ever do to deserve this damnation?" The wind swallows my words, but she giggles, her chin digging into my shoulder.

"I still don't know how you can make jokes with such a straight face." She leans back, holding me at arm's length. "It's actually quite frightening."

Abby rolls up her window and then turns to Bailey. "Are we even sure she's capable of laughing?" Her eyes widen and her lips form an 'O'. "Or smiling? I don't think we've seen you smile in years."

Bailey laces her fingers through mine and squeezes. "That's an exaggeration." She leans forward and grabs Abby's face, so she has fish lips. "Turn back around or I won't tell you about the lifeguard."

Abby gasps. "What lifeguard?" Bailey motions to the front seat. "Fine," Abby turns and crosses her arms over her chest. "I'll be good. But please tell me you got laid. Or at least felt up."

Bailey releases a throaty chuckle and turns to me. I immediately pull one corner of my mouth up, a reflex more than anything else. Then I turn to look out the opposite window as Bailey recounts her spring break fling.

* * *

"So what did I miss?"

Bailey pulls me along beside her, both of us trying to keep pace with Abby who, surprisingly, can walk quite fast in five-inch heels. I scuff my vans on the sidewalk, careful not to step on gum or any stranded worms. The ground is covered in tiny puddles and I can't help but stare at my reflection in each one. We have to push past other students in order to get into the building, and inside all the voices echo off the metal lockers and white walls.

Jacklyn walks behind us, too busy studying flashcards to walk properly. "Well, for starters, Abby has been asked to the dance by six different people, who she promptly turned down with a flip of her hair and a very convincing apology."

"Hey!" Abby stops at her locker, glaring at Jacklyn from the corner of her eye. "You all know I'm waiting for Lucas to ask me. Ugh," She fans herself and smacks her glossy lips together. "I can't wait to get my hands on that fine-as-hell male specimen."

"Why can't you just ask him?" Jacklyn wraps a rubber band around her flashcards and neatly tucks them in the front flap of her messenger bag. She then pulls out a binder, a pen, and her overly organized daily planner.

"If I do that, I'll look desperate. And I don't do desperate."

Bailey clicks her tongue and pulls me into her side as the first warning bell rings and a crowd of students rush by. "How, exactly, does that make you desperate?"

Abby taps her chin and shrugs. "I don't know but I know the guys usually ask the girls. Not the other way around."

Jacklyn shakes her head, glancing up briefly from her color-coded organizer. "You are such a contradiction, Abby. I'm aware that that's the social 'norm,'" she attempts to make air

30

quotes but fumbles trying to balance her agenda. "But you're a strong, independent woman. You don't have to wait for a guy to ask you out." She looks at Abby before scribbling in the margins of her agenda.

"Exactly." Bailey nods and gives Abby a thumbs up. "Just walk up to Lucas and use that heavy-hitter confidence you use on the diamond! Or are you scared he'll turn you down?"

Abby groans, running her palms over her hair to smooth down the frizz. "As if. But maybe..." She pulls on the hem of her V-neck tee. "Can I just show a little cleavage? To give him some incentive?"

"That's not an incentive, that's an offering." Bailey readjusts her book bag's straps as the second bell rings, a shrill sound that echoes off the crudely painted lockers.

"An offer he cannot refuse." Abby winks and saunters off, hip swaying with just enough exaggeration.

Bailey and I head to AP U.S. History, a class that always puts me to sleep. Not because it's boring, but because it's first period.

Before entering the class, I clear my throat and tug on Bailey's hand. "Did Jack ask you to the dance yet?"

She tilts her head back to release a sigh. "No, I have a feeling he won't. I mean, we're not officially dating, and I did just hook up with a random guy, but I mean... we're obviously interested in one another, right?" She shakes her head. "I don't have a problem asking him, but I also don't want to ruin whatever it is we are, you know?"

I nod, even though I don't. While everyone else has been obsessing over what color dress to wear and if their hair should be curled or pinned up, I've been worrying about the constant storms. Perhaps the Mayans were wrong about 2012, but 2019 could be the beginning of the end.

I can't find the energy to worry about heels, dangly earrings, or the perfect shade of lipstick. I definitely don't have the energy to worry about boys. But my silent sentiments don't resonate with the rest of the student body and I can't evade their prying questions.

Bailey is no exception and when we're both settled into our seats, she turns to me with a wide, wobbly smile. "Has anyone asked you to the dance? I would know if you were interested in someone."

I slowly shake my head and bite my lip as more students file into the classroom. "I don't necessarily exist at this school, Bailey."

She frowns, fumbling around inside her bag. "That's not true. You're just quiet and that's not a bad thing." She hands me a tiny composition notebook, the cover decorated with leaves and budding tulips. "They want you to try journaling since you don't want to see Dr. Kurtis anymore. It's their only condition." She tilts her head to the left, pursing her lips. "I'm not sure they'll actually check it, but I really think it could help you."

I stare at her, then at the notebook. I quickly flip through the lined pages, white and crisp with a sterilized smell. I place it in the center of my desk: a disturbing addition to my usually ordered routine.

I swallow a pint of saliva. "Who are "they"?"

"Your parents."

"You mean my mom." It's not a question and we both know it.

Bailey taps the cover, giving me a small smile. "It's just so you can keep your thoughts and feelings in one place. It may help you sort through where you are in recovery." I notice her voice drop an octave, but I can't tell if it's to keep our conversation private or if she's embarrassed.

"Where am I?" I can't stop staring at the notebook, wondering why my mom chose to give me this one specifically. I pick it up again and turn it over in my hands, looking for any blemishes. Bailey puts her hand on mine and I can't help but pull back, the notebook falling into my lap.

"You're the only one who can answer that."

I sit on my hands, their trembling making my entire body shake. I try to make eye contact, but my eyes are blurry. "When did you even have time to talk to them? My mom isn't even in town and dad has been MIA for months."

"They mailed this to me with a letter. You haven't been answering their phone calls." She suddenly reaches toward my leg and I flinch, not realizing that the notebook is on the floor. I grip the edge of my shirt.

"Right... phone calls. Dad hasn't called me, though." He has ignored my existence for what feels like forever. I sit back and place the notebook back in the center of my desk, fighting the urge to cover my ears as the last bells rings. "Class is starting."

"Oh, I almost forgot. You have to go to the nurse during lunch," She whispers to me, her mouth set in a hard, straight line and her eyes furrowed.

I try my best to concentrate as Ms. Jacob outlines the class agenda. I ball both my hands into fists, trying to stop them from shaking. The white board looms in front of me, large and clear for only a moment before everything goes dark.

I can still hear Ms. Jacob talk about women's suffrage but there is only blank space in front of me. I turn to my left, where Bailey should be, fingers wrapped lightly around a colored pen and her eyes trained on the board. But she's not there. The walls of the classroom are gone and darkness envelops me. I've been here before, in this void, and nothing ever happens. It's like I'm weightless, floating in space yet not really moving.

When I finally come to, students are shuffling out of the classroom and Bailey is packing up my bag. I grab the journal before she can touch it.

She sighs, pushing in her chair. "You went dark. I'll make a copy of my notes for you as long as you go to the nurse."

I slowly shake my head, slipping the journal into my bag and following her out of the class. "What are they going to do? Take my blood pressure?"

She slows down and pulls out her phone, fingers tapping rapidly against the screen. She slides the phone into her back pocket and lightly grabs my arm. "Have you been eating?"

I pull away from her. The question makes my skin itch and I pull my hands inside my jacket, gripping the rough fabric. "You always ask that. Of course I am. But I sleep through most meals."

Bailey stops and I run into her back. Her eyes run the length of my body, possibly looking for any visible skin impairments, before lacing her fingers through mine. "I thought you looked thin."

I shrug. "I haven't lost any weight."

She grunts, "So you say." She stops in front of the photography classroom just as the bell rings and pulls me in briefly for a hug. "We'll talk about this at lunch. Text me if you need me to come pick you up from class." She shoos me into the room.

I pull the door shut behind me, letting my shoulders loosen in the dim light and chemical fragrance emitted from developing photos. The dark room is tucked into the back of the

34

classroom, its red light on and signaling that the blacked-out door should remain closed.

I wait for the light to turn green and the photos to be taken out by their owner before shutting myself inside. I don't have any pictures to develop but I flip the light switch back to red anyway. I curl into a corner, rest my head on my bag, and close my eyes, the red tinted darkness a perfect lullaby.

There is a field of emerald grass that sways to the inaudible tune of the spring breeze. Sapphire buds pop up between the blades of grass, little pods of waxy petals and pollen just waiting to unfold. When I bend down to touch the buds, fingers shaking in anticipation, a breeze fills my nose with the scent of metal. It's strong enough to make my eyes burn but I breathe it in. The breeze stalls and each blade of grass stands still. Suddenly, the vibrant blue hue of the pods fades into a dull grey and the sun, which shone bright even behind the marshmallow clouds, gets snuffed out.

I open my eyes, not expecting the darkness to overtake even my dreams. The dark room is cold and my body is sore, the cement floor an upward pressure on my bones. I stand and stretch my body, trailing my hand along the wall in hopes of absorbing the red light's heat. I flip the light to green and step out.

Every light is on and the brightness makes me head spin. I pull my hood over my head, squeezing my eyes shut for a moment. The students are gone and Mr. Knaught, noticing me as I shuffle to the door, hands me a yellow manila folder. I slide it into my bag and pull out my phone and the journal. I have six texts from Bailey and Abby. I ignore them, reposition my bag on my shoulder, and head to the cafeteria.

I stay close to the lockers, trying to stay as small as possible.

The hallway is loud and smells of burnt meat. The journal is pressed against my chest and its corners dig into my skin. I stop a few feet from the cafeteria, taking deep whiffs of singed beef. Vomit churns in my stomach and tries climbing up my throat but I force it back down.

I text Bailey, telling her I feel sick and am going to lie down in the nurse's office. But I head back to the dark room, journal and pen in hand. When the red light goes on, I fit myself into a corner and write about my dream.

I write about the darkness.

Pocket Full of Daises

Aryn

I can never stop myself from hesitating on my porch, the front door a warm mahogany that welcomes me with open arms. But the unquestionable acceptance of the house is what creates a tight fist in my stomach. My throat closes and I blink back tears. I press my palms against my eyelids and take a deep breath before opening the door.

The house is always filled to the brim with sweetened scents of blueberry muffins and chamomile tea. It warms my skin as I take in deep whiffs. There is never silence here: always gentle voices, high-pitched giggles, the relentless soft clicking of a keyboard, and the ragged snoring of my younger sister. The noise is quiet and thoughtful, drastically different than what usually fills my head. I try to take advantage of the reprieve from the harsh, unforgiving words that smash against the side of my skull on a daily basis. The words that ricochet and penetrate every hidden crevice until they become all I know; I own them, I said them, I believe them.

Sometimes I expect the house to echo back the words and

I cringe, bracing myself for their impact. But every harsh syllable is smothered by gentle whispers and soft hands. I don't always hear my own panicked breathing, I don't always feel empty.

But when the house is empty, its bones shake. I cannot walk up the stairs without my footsteps landing heavy on the old floorboards and making them creak in anxiety. I cannot walk through the trembling house without being reminded of all the things this family has gone through. All the things I have done.

I climb the stairs two at a time, running my hands along the walls, feeling the peeling wallpaper. I try not to look at the various photos hung up, snapshots of the past that make me breathless. My fingers graze a frame and the corner digs into my nail. I snatch my hand back and stick my thumb into my mouth, running my tongue over the coppery liquid as I try to put the photo back in place.

The frame feels weird in my grasp, like it shouldn't be touched. I can feel the familiar tight swirls that are deeply etched in the grooves around the border. I finger the two sets of initials; both ending in C. I squeeze my eyes shut. My pulse slows and suddenly it's too quiet in this snug house.

I try as gently as I can to place the photo back onto its hook, evening it out when it wobbles too far to the left. The stairs seem unstable now as I climb them, and I hesitate to inhale and exhale before stepping. They seem to scream in protest, begging me to leave them alone. I beg them to leave *me* alone. Their screams only get louder.

Plush carpet cushions my fall and I bury my face into the flooring. I try to breathe deep, my fingers aching from trying to hold on. The screams start to fade. I push myself away from the safety of solid ground and head to my room.

Aside from the occasional strewn pair of socks and boxers, my room is spotless. I keep it in pristine condition so my mom doesn't have a reason to come in. I rarely let anyone in my room: it's the only place where I don't have to pretend.

I slide the blue polo over my head and shiver as the cold air hits my chest, stinging like someone just pressed a hundred tacks into me. The cool mattress conforms to my figure, pulling me in. The ceiling is a hideous shade of tan, worn out and covered in cracks. I close my eyes but can't erase the images and sounds: the hand-carved frame, the screams, the last goodbye I never got to bid. They run again and again through my head. I press my balled-up fists to my eyes, trying to block out hospital bills, a blue, plastic breathing machine, tired, frightened brown eyes.

I run my hands over my chest, fingering the welts I put there. It's been so long since I've felt that kind of pain and sometimes, I honestly believe the pain is the only way I can go on. But I've stopped with the lighters, stopped with the slow burn.

My therapist used to emphasize the saying "forgive and forget." Forgetting seems more feasible. I can shove the memories back and hide them behind a thick wall. But of course, that's only temporary. They push and push until all the bricks come tumbling down. And then I just rebuild, waiting patiently for the dam to flood, over and over again.

*   *   *

I feel like I'm going to burst. The soft hum of the air conditioner feels like electricity. The house, though not exactly quiet, is empty. My mother should be home with my sister at any moment and I should be downstairs, waiting for them at the door. But I can't look either of them in the eye, can't even breathe because I feel that if I do, these walls will be torn down and all that will be left is rubble.

I started dinner: put sauce and meatballs on a low flame and boil water for the noodles. The timer is on, a persistent ticking that almost lulls me to sleep. It almost sounds like a heart monitor, steady and reassuring until it gets to zero. And this is the difference. You can always set the timer again, you can always have more time. A heart monitor doesn't give you that option.

I hear the door open and my sister's squeal of excitement. Cartoon Network is turned on and the volume is turned up. I'm sitting against the back of the couch, which faces the kitchen, so of course Allie doesn't notice me, although I doubt she'd choose me over a rerun of The Amazing World of Gumball anyway. My mom walks by me, my presence blending into the furniture. I count to ten and then tiptoe to the kitchen, imagining the floor crumbling under my weight and taking everyone down with me.

My mom is stirring the sauce in slow, methodic movements. The urge to hug her makes my pulse quicken. Instead, I grab the saltshaker and pour a handful into the boiling water beside her. She jumps, eyes wide and her right hand splayed against her chest.

"Aryn! Jeez, don't do that." She takes a deep breath, squeezing my shoulder. Her eyes flicker to my bare chest. "Thank you for starting dinner. I'm starving."

I nod, pulling out bowls and forks and setting the table. I stand awkwardly behind my mom as she sorts through the mail, eyebrows furrowed in concentration.

"Can you stay down here and watch this for me so I can take a shower? I'll only be ten minutes."

I nod, stirring the sauce as she walks out of the room. Then I go into the living room, sitting directly behind Allie as she sways to the characters singing. She still hasn't noticed me but I can't relax, closing my eyes and bracing myself for the moment she turns around.

Finally, there's a commercial and I hear her excited intake of breath and her tiny feet running across the carpet.

"Aryn!" She screams, throwing herself onto my lap and wrapping her thin arms around my neck. I squeeze her, smoothing down her frizzy hair and inhaling her cherry lollipop scent. She leans back to look at me and I freeze.

My eyes are immediately drawn to the pink, puckered skin that starts from the tip of her chin and extends to the bottom of her right ear, stretching the ivory skin that surrounds it. Underneath her shirt, extending down her right arm, is more burned skin. Already, people have asked her questions and stared. She doesn't really remember what happened, doesn't know that she could've died. But that's not what makes me flinch and avert my eyes.

It's her eyes that strike a low blow to my sanity. Her big, doe eyes without a doubt bear a resemblance to his: chocolate brown rimmed with gold. Her thick lashes flutter against her hooded eyelids, perfectly shaped under thin eyebrows. She is a carbon copy of him and a constant reminder of how much of a fuck up I am.

I want to hate her, blame her for taking my happiness away, for leaving me vulnerable and resentful, but we all know it's not her fault. And when she flashes those dark rimmed eyes at me, I'm defenseless.

"Aryn?" I grasp the couch, resisting the impulse to stare. I can feel her eyes on my face, silently begging me to look at her, accept her. "I need to tell you something *very, very* important!" She adds extra emphasis, pleading.

Sighing, I turn my head slightly towards her, running my eyes over her hopeful face. She squeals when I place my hands beneath her armpits and place her more firmly onto my lap, wrapping my arms around her small frame.

"What is it, Allie?" I ask, my voice wavering on her name. I just barely notice the pink that spreads across her plush cheeks as she digs her face into my bare chest, her warmth seeping in and dulling the chill. My scars, her scars, never seem to bother her. "What is it?" I repeat, anxiety coating my words; I automatically fear the worst.

"I don't know what to do!" She suddenly yells, leaning away from me. "Listen, okay? And don't interrupt." She turns her big, watery eyes unto me and again, my eyes start to drift downwards. But I focus on the curiosity gleaming in her eyes, welcoming the distraction. I tilt my head down just an inch and she takes that as a yes.

Allie averts her eyes and admits, "There's this boy…" Her voice is soft. "I'm still not sure if I like boys but he sits next to me in class and always gives me half of his cookie during lunch. He's really funny! And he made me something…" She whispers, reaching into her pocket.

I can't help but smile as she produces a poorly crafted handmade ring consisting of daisies. And somehow, her ignorance relaxes me. I can feel myself un-tensing as she tries to fit the ring on her pinky, though it's obviously way too big. I chuckle, carefully sliding it off and placing it on her ring finger.

"It seems like someone has a crush on you." I tease, amused by her wide eyes.

"He… likes me?" Her cheeks darken to a scarlet tint, spreading across her entire face and clashing against the pink scar.

I rest my chin on the crown of her head. She presses her face up against my bare chest and tucks it under my neck. I tug on her pigtails, earning an angelic giggle.

"So who's the lucky guy?"

"His name is Franklin and he is 8." She twirls the ring around her finger, again and again.

"Ah, an older man, eh? And he made you that?" I ask, pointing to the ring.

She smiles up at me. "Yeah, I'm going to wear it forever and never take it off. That's how much I love it. Do you like it?" I nod, as usual calmed by her innocence. Will it fade as she gets older? Will she, too, learn to hate me?

"If we get married, I hope we get along good. Like mom and daddy did." My grip tightens.

"I don't know if I love Franklin. But to get married you should be in love, right? Franklin is nice but well, I think," she lowers her voice to a whisper. "I think he has cooties!" She giggles into my ear. I squeeze my eyes, trying to block out her voice. "Mom and daddy loved each other, didn't they?"

"Yes, they-" My voice is hoarse. The welts begin to pulse. "Yes," I repeat. "They loved each other very much."

I can feel her smile. "I guess daddy didn't have cooties because mommy loved him and married him."

"She still loves him." I whisper, trying to keep the venom from lacing its way around the four, overly simple words. I lift her off my lap and set her down in front of the TV. "Finish watching Gumball. Dinner will be done soon."

I don't look at her as I walk away but I can feel her stare. I curl my fingers into a fist and stand in front of the bubbling sauce, little air pockets exploding and sending sauce flying onto my chest.

I bury my face in my hands, stopping the tears before they even have the chance to escape. I am weak. Easily and utterly destroyed by just a few words, by a past I can never escape.

I can feel my body shake with the effort to keep myself from falling apart. My ribs hurt. I feel like screaming. Hitting something. My throat clogs up, my heart beats like a drum in my chest and echoes up into my ears.

I turn the burners off and drain the noodles. Steam rises and I have to close my eyes as memories assault me. I gulp a glass of water, and then another, trying to quench the dry expanse of my throat and put out the fire in my stomach.

Obsidian Eyes

Savannah

There is nothing to be gained by having the house to yourself. There are too many shadows and creaking floorboards. There is too much silence that invites paranoia and restless sleep. Even if my parents do sell this house, the next one will be just as empty.

Walking into the house is like walking into a freezer. I sigh when I notice all the windows are closed and white clouds sneak out from between my lips. I head to the fridge, where the post-it note screaming "OPEN WINDOWS" in bright red sharpie remains untouched. I crumple it up then rub my hands down my arms, soothing the goosebumps. The windows stick and by the time they are all open on the ground floor, my hands are raw and sweat lightly coats my face.

As I step back into the living room, the sweat cools. Even with the warm breeze blowing in, my bones shutter and my ribs ache from shaking. I reposition my bag and head for the stairs. They are padded and swallow my steps, silencing my presence and sending a resounding hush throughout the house.

When I reach the top I hesitate, eyes travelling the length of the hallway and scanning for any sign of life other than my own beating heart and chilled breath.

I take slow, measured steps and avoid the closed doors. I feel so closed off from the bones and organs of the house; why can't I hear its lungs through the vents? Are the creaking floorboards its pulse? The only open door leads to the bathroom, its porcelain and chrome finishings exposed under a tiny chandelier made of crystals. I continue, pulling my arms into my sides. I'm almost to my room when I notice a small streak of light. The hair on my arms stand erect.

I haven't seen the inside of my parents' room in almost ten years. When I was little, it was my playground. I would camp out under the sheets, pretending to be out in the wild hunting lions. Or I would dress up in my mom's pearls and high heels, eager to grow into her organized wardrobe. I was small enough to hide underneath the bed and when I had nightmares my parents would let me sleep between them, snuggled up to both of their sides.

But then the nightmares decided to latch onto me and they never went away. My so-called protectors couldn't deal with the frequent disturbances in their sleep patterns. In the end, my haven was just a lie.

Now my parents' door is slightly cracked, sucking in a small sliver of the light spread across the hallway. Before I know it, my hand is wrapped around the tarnished bronze handle. I follow the thin strip of light that breaks through the darkness. Shadows stick to the walls like silent guards. I can almost see their black eyes staring back at me. My grip tightens on the handle, the smooth round surface slipping beneath my sweaty palm and I pull the door closed.

But their eyes still haunt me.

I continue down the hallway but again, I pause. I am exhausted and feel the magnetic pull of my padded mattress. I step inside the doorframe, ready to drop and doze, but immediately feel the ice. I imagine sliding beneath the comforter and pulling the covers of my head. Taking a deep breath and curling into a ball. The mattress would conform to my body, but the cold would only seep further into my bones.

I cross the hallway, my thighs thick and frozen. They rub against each other like sandpaper, heavy as lead. The red tinted room beckons me, and I willingly shroud myself in its dim light and metallic scents.

This dark room, slightly smaller than the one at school because it used to be my nursery, is where I spend most of my time. It was a gift from my oh-so-loving parents for my 16th birthday and I almost muttered the three forbidden words. But my throat tightened and all I could think about were the years of broken promises and silent apologies stuffed into 1,000 dollars of remodeling.

And yet, the red light and the smell of nickels does not comfort me today. The walls close in on me and I can't seem to find the door, although I never closed it. I turn in circles, round and round like a coin on its edge, until the room is spinning all on its own.

Finally, I burst into the hallway and take in huge gulps of stale air. My lungs burn. I clutch my chest and run down the stairs, hastily slipping on flip flops, and rush out the door.

The sun immediately licks my skin and I roll my shoulder blades. Throwing my head back, I relish in the clear sky and walk into the woods lining the driveway. Overgrown trees try hiding the sun and create flashing lights, like the sporadic technicolor beams in a nightclub. The overgrown shrubs cover the majority of the ground and mounds of dirt serve as humble abodes to hiding creatures, but I can walk the path with my eyes closed.

Because I know the path to him. He's the epitome of perfection: his waxy petals don crystal droplets that reflect the setting sun, accompanied by their own personal halos. He has a proud stature and it is admirable how he can stand so tall against the green blades that swim below him. How he can snub the crowd questioning his sanity.

There are hundreds of kaleidoscope flowers that sparkle like recently discovered gems. They come in groups of red, yellow, and white but he flaunts his own shade of beauty; the lone blue gemstone that shines the brightest unintentionally, oblivious to my wandering eye.

I sit on a mossy stump near him, breathing in the light-soaked air. Rays from the sun fill my lungs, swirling and expanding. I can feel my heart throbbing, pushing against my chest in an attempt to touch his soft spine.

I love these moments – isolated and surrounded by dense foliage and flickering shadows. I embrace these moments of solitude and the darkness that engulfs me from a place outside my own body. I love the unknown dangers that prowl beyond my field of visions and the sense of immunity this obliviousness seems to emit.

I pull my knees up to my chest, exhaling through my nose and digging my nails into my shins.

"Sometimes I don't know what to do with myself."

It's barely a whisper but I know he hears me; I can almost feel him whisper in my ear to keep speaking. My lips tremble as liquid salt drips down my face and into my mouth. I taste every word I have never said.

"I'm defunct. They keep shoving pills down my throat." I feel the tears resting in my collar bone and they're cold, like tiny icicles. "They're trying to fix me, but I don't... I don't know what's wrong with me."

I force a laugh up my throat and out my parched lips, scrubbing the tears away. Or maybe rubbing them into my skin. "That's a lie. Everything is wrong with me. This body and this brain –"

He bends over, his bud tipping in a silent apology. I choke back a sob and touch the silver pendant around my neck. It's strangling me, the ribbon stamped onto the metal coiling around my throat. I crawl next to him and lean against a neighboring tree. I dig my fingers into the soil.

As the sun sets to my horizon, I only notice the silhouettes of individual petals. Shadows lurking in the darkness. A tingling sensation spreads from my wrist to my fingertips, numb from the constant grip on my shins.

I reach for his stem as if it was a hand and let the darkness in.

Wild One

Aryn

Another restless night.

I'm tracing the cracks in the window when the morning light digs its claws into my face and begs me to get out of bed. I open my mouth and try to swallow the warmth, the staggering bursts of cold air freezing my insides. I squirm around the bed, rolling my shoulders and arching my back until I hear a series of tiny pops.

The smell of dark roast coffee grabs fistfuls of my numb nerves, massaging the life back into them. My lips involuntarily curve upward, the aroma invoking snapshots of blissful family weekends.

I dangle my feet off the edge of the bed and shiver as the cold hardwood seeps into my soles. Goosebumps scatter along my nude arms and legs.

I drag my drowsy body to the shower, standing under the spray until my skin is raw and red. Hating the prospect of cold coffee, I take the steps two at a time. My mom sits at the table, hiding behind her laptop with her right hand permanently attached to a coffee mug, steam rising in delicious swirls. She types away, seemingly oblivious to my presence until I swallow a mouthful of my own combination of caffeine, sugar cubes, and hazelnut creamer and groan.

"Oh god, I burnt my tongue." I rub the tip of my tongue against my teeth as my mom rolls her eyes over the rims of her glasses. "But so good." I proceed to down the entire mug and then mix another.

"You're up early."

I swish the last remnants of my coffee around and nod, even though she hasn't lifted her head once. "Couldn't sleep."

Allie's soft snores reach my ears and I venture into the living room to see her sprawled out on the couch; tiny feet clad in pink socks with frills. Her auburn hair sticks to her face in clumps of sweat and deep breaths rack her chest. I tuck her hair behind her ears and push her away from the edge of the couch, inhaling her scent of candy and shampoo.

"Long night?" I ask when I reenter the kitchen. I rinse my cup in the sink and then place it, among other dirty plates and utensils, into the dishwasher.

"Yeah," She lets loose a long sigh, finally looking up at me. I see the bags under her eyes and the wrinkles in her brow. "Allie was too wired and woke up at four. I'm surprised you didn't hear her running around the house." A content smile flits across her face before she stands, handing me her mug, only tiny grains of coffee left behind.

I watch as she turns in a circle, as if forgetting something, before tucking her laptop under her arm. I want to speak to her, about anything, but her silence makes my fingers twitch. I walk into the foyer and start lacing up my sneakers, rotating my ankles until they crack.

"Going for a run?" My mom yells from the kitchen, momentarily forgetting the dozing toddler on the couch.

I nod, reaching down to touch my toes. "I'll be back in like 15. Then I'll make Allie breakfast." I open the door and, without waiting for a response, run off the porch and into the surrounding woods as if the house just burst into flames. Again.

The sound of my feet hitting pavement is silenced as I jog into the dirt expanse of the woods. The pressure in my bones and the thin coat of perspiration accumulating on my neck fills me with purpose, so that when I get to the end of my property, the invisible boundary I know so well, I continue running.

This is unchartered territory and the specks of sunlight littering the clumps of grass makes me dizzy. I force my legs to propel my sluggish body forward. Tiny bursts of color start to pop up from the sparse weeds and thin dirt. It reminds me of a color wheel – red, yellow, and white endlessly spinning.

But then there is one lone explosion of blue. So vibrant and unexpected I lose both my breath and my footing. I hold onto a tree to balance myself, chest heaving. This shade of blue knocks a memory loose in my head, but it stays hidden, shoved in the back with all the things I choose to forget. But I want to know this blue, so I take a step forward, trying to inspect the oddity, and then I see her.

She is curled into a ball at the base of a tree, just a few feet away from the aqua colored tulip, as if guarding its existence. Her appearance is just a crumpled mesh of dark denim, bare arms, and frizzy hair. I feel my pulse quicken and my feet move of their own accord.

Fifteen steps later I smell her: a strange combination of blueberries and topsoil. Her hair is a deep chestnut, one long braid that hangs over her shoulder and spills tiny tendrils. Her tank top dips low, cleavage hugging a thin silver chain. I reach out a shaky hand, inches from her shoulder, when I realize her breath is ragged. Her outstretched hand is clenched into a fist.

I want to look closer, but she moans, a soft mew that pulls her facial features in. Her mouth is plump and pink, nose a shiny bulb, and her forehead, scrunched up at the moment, is littered with minuscule blemishes. The way her face is pinched with pain finally sets my chest on fire: she's having a nightmare.

I poke her shoulder but she shifts away from me, creating a tiny wall of dirt and leaves behind her. I bend down, but before I can study her face in more detail, her eyes snap open and I'm sucked into a darkness I'm not sure I want to escape. Her eyes are a deep brown, like the damp soil beneath her and her pupils are nearly invisible. They widen for just a moment before her entire face relaxes.

I expect her to punch me or at least scream, but she just opens her mouth and whispers, "Hi." I'm so shocked by her innocent greeting that I'm not even bothered by the soft scent of morning breath.

I take a few steps back as she starts to lift herself off the ground, carefully removing any leaves or clumps of dirt. As she straightens her shirt, I can't help but trail the length of her body and notice that her toes are painted almost the same exact shade of blue as the tulip. But then she stops moving, silently demanding my undivided attention. We stare at one another, only a few feet apart. Then it hits me; this is the girl from the cafeteria! Now that she isn't staring at me from across the room, her gaze, although intense, doesn't seem as creepy. Whatever I felt that day during lunch is coming back full force.

"Why are you staring at me? Is there something on my face?" Her voice is smooth, and I lean forward, trying to catch the ends of her words. She runs her fingers down her face and then through her hair, shaking out dead leaves.

I think I have indigestion. My chest is still on fire so I press my palm there, light and fast like burping a baby. She continues to look at me, eyes wide.

"Why were you sleeping out here?"

She shrugs, but then points to the blue tulip, as if all the questions in the world could be answered simply by looking at it.

"Aren't your parents worried about you? Do they know where you are?"

She shakes her head slowly, like the question doesn't really make sense. "I belong to the house and it to me." It doesn't make sense, but I can't question her quick enough before she looks up at the sunlight playing peek-a-boo with the trees and spreads her arms out wide. I clear my throat, equally confused and intrigued. She stops, her eyes barreling into me, and takes a step forward. "Who are you?"

"Aryn Cooper." I point behind me, indicating the way to my house. "I live on the other side."

"You're my neighbor?" She tilts her head to the side, her body following suit. "I didn't know we had neighbors." Her voice trails off as her eyes close and she starts to sway, as if off balance.

I rush towards her with my arms poised to catch her. I don't touch her but I'm so close I can see an eyelash on her cheek. "Hey, are you alright?"

She touches her forehead, then leans it against my shoulder as if the weight of it is too much. I can't help but tense up. I feel her chest heave. "Yes," she mumbles, pulling away. "I'm sorry. I'm fine." She grips the chain around her neck.

And then she smiles at me, lips pulled tight across white teeth – one further back then all the others – and my mouth is filled with saliva. I have to swallow three times before I know for sure that I'm not going to drool. But I can see her jaw clenching and unclenching, the muscles twitching with the effort, and I force myself to move away.

"You go to Griffin, right?"

She nods, a curt movement of the head. "Junior."

I press my hand against my chest again. "Me too. I've only seen you once, though, which is weird."

"That's actually not surprising." She doesn't explain, just glances at me. "I've never seen you before." Her voice is dull and her words are clipped. Does she not remember staring at me in the cafeteria then?

I see a lone fallen leave tangled in her braid and take a step forward. Her entire posture changes, like my movement just flipped a switch. She looks behind me and then at her feet as they propel her backwards. "I should probably go. Get ready for school and stuff."

I don't understand why my chest hurts, why the fire hasn't been put out yet. But as she turns around, her braid a thick rope against her back, I panic.

"Wait! Uhm, do you need a ride or something?" My voice cracks and I want to sink into the ground.

She pauses but doesn't turn back around. Her shoulders are slumped and, somehow, I can imagine a storm in those muddy eyes. She moves her head slowly to the left and then to the right and disappears into the dense bushes leading to her house.

I stare after her for only a moment before looking at the blue enigma, surrounded by dark soil and damaged leaves. A few seconds later and I'm jogging back the way I came, trailing along a sparking wildfire and a hollow sound echoing in my chest.

Silence

Savannah

"Something happened this weekend."

Two pairs of eyes the color of hazelnuts immediately turn to me.

"What?" Bailey tugs my hand to her chest and starts inspecting my arm. "What did you do?"

I pull my hand away and capture it between my thighs. "I didn't do anything. It's just, I was in the woods-"

"Whoa, wait!" Abby points her index finger at me. "Why were you in the woods by yourself?"

Judging by the tone in her voice, it's best not to mention the fact that I sleep out there most nights. So instead, I lift my shoulders until they meet my ears. "Just taking a walk."

"You need to be careful, Sav." Jacklyn pipes up from the driver's seat, glancing briefly at me in the rearview mirror.

I take a deep breath and glance out the window. Every time I open my mouth, my words get sucked out and devoured. I try again, coaxing my throat and tongue to push out a string of letters and sounds. "Anyway, I was walking and there was this boy. We didn't talk much but-"

"Boy?!" Abby screeches and her eyebrows rise until they disappear beneath her neatly trimmed bangs. "Let me get my bat."

I lean back in my seat and tip my head until my neck feels like it's going to snap. But I continue, because this faceless boy followed me all the way back to my house. I couldn't see his eyes, but I knew he was watching me as I rinsed off all the soil in the shower. I knew he could hear my footsteps echo throughout the house and knew he questioned why the house was cold and empty. But he never spoke. Not one word.

"Apparently, he's my neighbor." I close my eyes and try to recall his voice. "His name is Aryn, same grade as us."

I can still feel their eyes on me but I'm staring at the felt ceiling of Jacklyn's jeep, trying to remember the shape of his mouth and the feel of his fingers on my shoulder. It is rare that I meet a stranger and remember them.

"His name sounds familiar." Abby has all but crawled into the backseat with Bailey and me. "Was he cute?"

I rack my brain for a moment, trying to remember the way his mouth moved, how his hands looked. "I don't know."

"Huh," Bailey forehead creases. "I'm pretty sure he's in the other Gov. class. I've seen him talking to Ms. Jacob."

Jacklyn pulls into the school parking lot, her jeep fitting snug between a minivan and an SUV. "Yes, and he also dated Clara when you guys were freshmen." She turns off the ignition and meets my eyes in the rearview mirror again, shaking her head in a slow, precise movement. "Stay away from him, Savannah. He may not be a bad guy, but we all know that once Clara has sunk her claws into someone, they're her property. And she's not good with sharing."

Abby chuckles, finally returning to her seat. "You think she'd let someone at least rent the poor boy out?"

As we leave the car, I listen to them make jokes about Aryn as if he is nothing more than a piece of real estate. I can't help but wonder if he is the kind of property that is recently renovated, with no broken pipes or uneven foundation. Or if he is the old, haunted mansion wobbling on a hill, filled with secret passageways and skeletons in the closet.

* * *

"The dance is fast approaching, ladies! It's time to strategize!"

Abby's voice echoes off the lockers, loud and buoyant amidst the chaos in the hallway. She's the herder and we're her sheep and she leads us to a bathroom on the first floor, down the ramp and all the way in the back of the school. It's blocked by caution tape and my mind goes in millions of directions as to why; what could be so horrible that they had to seal it off?

I hold my breath as the weight of Abby's arm sinks into my bones. Her warm skin is such a contrast to the air pumping out of the vents. Her hip graces my thigh as she ducks under the tape and pushes open the door. I bite the inside of my cheek.

"The caution tape is unnecessary, really." Abby rolls her eyes as she leans us both up against a wall.

"Well," starts Jacklyn, burying her nose into her forearm. "Taking us to a closed bathroom is unnecessary. Why couldn't we just go to my car?"

Abby pouts and squeezes me to her side. "I wanted this to be our hideout."

I try to focus on the stench of the toilets and how they make

59

my head spin. I stare up at the brown freckled ceiling. I dig my nails into my palms. I focus on everything besides the warmth of Abby's skin again my icy slab of cells and tissue.

Bailey, as if sensing my inner turmoil, pulls Abby to the stalls. "You want our hideout to be a bathroom that still has remnants of bodily fluids? Look, that's not even pee!"

A groan escapes Abby's throat. "This is nothing compared to locker rooms, but fine. No hiding out in a bathroom. But since we're here, can we at least talk about dance preparations?" She throws us all puppy dog eyes.

Jacklyn hops up on one of the sinks, its porcelain shine tainted with rust and mold. "Why am I even here? I'm not a junior; I won't go to a junior dance."

"Oh god. Here comes the senior mentality we all know so well!"

"It's not a mentality, Abby. It's a simple fact."

"I want to be a senior." Bailey sags against the wall. "Junior year has been hell."

Jacklyn clicks her tongue. "No, you don't! College apps have slowly chipped away at my sanity. Stay young while you can."

"Hey!" Abby claps her hands together and the sound drills into my ears. "We are here to talk about dresses, shoes, and dates. Not college!"

"Whatever, continue."

"Good, good." A smirk spreads across Abby's face and she starts pacing. "We need to go dress shopping this weekend. Or tomorrow after school. We need to find Savannah a date and pool money together to rent a car nicer than Jacklyn's jeep."

Jacklyn protests, "Hey! There's nothing wrong with my car. But who said it was even an option?"

I turn into the wall while they're arguing and murmur a

quiet "I'm not going." They don't hear me so I repeat it again, forcing the words out with a sense of desperation. I just want them to listen to me.

Both Bailey and Abby turn to me, strained smiles on their face. "Of course you are." They don't bother asking me why I don't want to go because they already know.

They continue to argue about hairstyles and dress cuts, making decisions about times and eligible dates for me. And I'm ignored. Crammed into the grimy ceramic tiles where their voices dip hungrily into the compacted brown grime. I'm squished between the spotted mirrors and the broken tampon dispensers.

Their voices start weaving themselves around my brain. The air gets thicker and my saliva clogs my throat, sticking to the sides of my cheeks. The walls seem to breathe with me, labored and forced.

Warm hands grip my shivering frame and I'm jolted to reality. To the grime infested bathroom and the shrieking warning bell.

"Is that time alright with you, Sav?"

I'm not sure what I'm agreeing to, but I nod anyway, taking Bailey's hand and blinding following her to our next period. My feet don't seem to work and I can't stop yawning. When I find a seat, warm from the person before me, I can't help but place my head down on the desk and close my eyes.

This time, for reasons beyond my comprehension, Aryn is in the darkness with me.

Lost Girl

Aryn

"I met a girl."

Corey turns to look at me, sloppy joe hanging from his open mouth. He speaks around the seasoned meat, "Ah gwirl?"

I nod, picking the sesame seeds off my bun. "Well, met again. Kind of."

He doesn't even chew, just swallows the meat; I can see it travelling down his throat. "Anything like Clara?"

I shrug but then reconsider. "Definitely not. I was only with her for a few minutes, but she was so…" I run a hand through my hair, the words sticking to the tip of my tongue. "She was fucking sleeping in the woods behind my house, dude."

I have his full attention now. "Why was she in the woods? Is she, ya know," he brings his index finger to his temple and creates a circle. He whispers, "crazy?"

"She's my neighbor. And I don't think she's crazy."

Corey taps his chin, eyes darting back and forth as if solving an invisible equation. "I don't know anyone aside from you who lives up there. Very secluded, you sociopath." He winks at me and takes another huge bite from his bun. Meat splatters onto the table. "What did you mean when you said you met her again?"

I stare at the meat on the table. "She's the staring contest girl. From last week, remember?"

His eyes widen and he nods, struggling to swallow.

"Corey, I feel like I'm the one who's crazy. I can't stop thinking about her."

He pops one of my tater tots into his mouth, rapidly chewing and then gulps down a 20oz Cherry Pepsi. He wipes his mouth on his sleeve and then stands up, his chair scraping against the floor. He leans across the table. "I mean, she's pretty, right?"

I close my eyes and nod, imagining her red mouth and muddy eyes. Even covered in dirt and leaves, she was untouchable. "Yes, she is beautiful. But that's not why she's on my mind."

"Then why?"

I think back to those miniscule moments with her, sheltered from the sweltering sun by the thick overgrowth of trees. "She was so strange. I've never met anyone who willingly sleeps outside when they have a bed not even 100 feet away. And then she seemed to go through multiple personalities in the mere span of five minutes."

"Do you think she's being abused?"

"Oh god." My chest starts to spout smoke. "I don't..." Her wide, glossy eyes didn't necessarily scream for help, but she definitely seemed afraid of me. "I don't know. But she did look scared when she left."

"How so?" Corey leans even closer to me, his eyes probing. He wants to know the secret, wants to know why this girl acts the way she does. But I don't have the answers.

"When she left, she looked so…" I search for the right word to describe the look on her face as she ran from me. "Lost. It's hard to explain."

He nods once, then twice. He slides back into his seat, his eyes glazing over. I stab the last tater tot on my plate, reducing it to mere particles. "I'll ask around." He finally declares, pointing at me with that all too familiar glint in his eye.

"You'll what?"

He cackles, rubbing his palms together as he frantically scours the cafeteria. "I promise you this, Aryn." He holds out his pinky in front of my face. "I will find you your lost girl."

* * *

Aside from my family, it's always been Corey and me. Since third grade we've done literally everything together: family vacations, our own pity party sleepovers, trying out for the basketball team and missing every layup. When Corey was being bullied in seventh grade, I was the one who got a busted lip and three weeks suspension.

But when I was 14, and we both thought nothing tragic could ever really happen, my father died. I was so racked with guilt and rage that I stopped going to school, stopped talking to Corey and my mom and just receded into myself.

That was when I met Clara. She didn't ask about my father or my feelings. She just got on top of me and made me forget. She was intoxicating. Like a drug that keeps pulling you in, even though you want to quit, need to quit.

I was not the only one who had seen her body uncovered and unscripted. But she was beautiful for a while and I was obsessed with the way she could make me forget. Just a slip of her tongue made my eyes roll back and the memories of fire fade. Then I only focused on her rough skin and the sheets tangling around us.

But every time she kissed me goodbye, I would squeeze my eyes shut so tightly it hurt and imagine her as anyone else. When I was sure she was gone, I would get under the covers and stare out the window. The sun would be setting, the sky turning a light pink. The forest behind my house would cast dark figures across the ground. I never saw the house on the opposite side but always knew it was there.

This only lasted a few months into my freshmen year before Corey finally had enough.

"You're a little bitch!" He screamed one day after school. There were tears in his eyes and I had to look away. "You can't just push me away."

I tried walking past him, tried ignoring the knot in my chest. But he tackled me to the ground, fists making contact with my ribs and jaw. I just let him hit me, the taste of blood filling my mouth.

"She's not good for you! She's taking advantage of your grief and we made a promise, you bastard!" His tears fell into my mouth and I swallowed. "I know that you hate yourself for what happened," He whispered, pulling himself off me and lying on the cement beside me. "But I need to be included in the pity party. I tried to RSVP but you never even sent me an invitation."

I couldn't respond. I couldn't apologize for trying to destroy myself because that's what I thought I deserved. We just lay there, my jaw sore and his eyes puffy. And from that moment on, I knew that as long as Corey was there to knock some sense into me, I'd never truly be alone.

Mirage

Savannah

"When is your mom coming back?"

I shrug, fingering a rack of halter top gowns covered in frills. "Soon, I guess."

Abby stares at my reflection in the mirror, her fingers gripping the shimmering material of her semi-see-through dress. "You guess? Doesn't she tell you her schedule?"

She turns toward me and the glare of multicolored sequins penetrates my line of vision. I press my palms against my eyelids, eager to dislodge the burst of colors.

"Not always." I respond, plopping down into one of the feather stuffed chairs. "Sometimes she just comes," I lift my fisted hands into the air, "and goes. Poof!" I let them drop back down into my lap.

Abby shakes her head in my general direction, tucking loose strands behind an ear. "She has serious issues, Sav. And don't even get my started with your dad. I think I actually prefer my parents." She squints her eyes. "And you know how overzealous they get."

I get distracted by the flickering florescent bulbs, piled awkwardly on top of one another to resemble a chandelier. I stare at the collage of glass until my eyes burn and I have to blink away the tears.

Abby's phone starts ringing, the painful tones of Taylor Swift's *Bad Blood* bouncing off the mirrors and punching me in the face. Abby holds up one finger.

"Hello?" She nods, turning to me and rolling her eyes. "Where the hell are you guys? We're been here for like twenty minutes." She starts examining her fingers, bruised and scarred from long days practicing. "Yeah, whatever. Just get here." She throws her phone onto the seat next to me and I watch as it bounces to the floor.

As I pick it up, the plastic case slipping through my fingers, Abby twirls in front of the three-way mirror. Her olive skin glows a faint pink under the glistening chandelier.

"Does this dress look okay?" She turns to me with her pink mouth pursed. "I don't know about the bust." She cups her breasts so that they spill out over the sweetheart neckline.

I open my mouth to speak but inhale a lump of glitter and cinnamon incense. For the first time, I notice how the whole room is shadowed in rosy hues and tiny crystals hang from every other tile in the ceiling; the bulb chandelier rests in the center. One version of my personal hell.

"I like it."

"That's all? You don't think it's too much?"

I pull my legs into my chest. "I mean, it's see-through."

"And?"

"I can see your underwear."

She sputters, her eyes wide as she struts up to me. "That's so embarrassing! Why didn't you tell me sooner?" She pulls the dress up to her knees and extends a leg. Then she groans and flops down into the chair next to me. "This is all so stressful. I know I like shopping and dressing up, but dances cause too much pressure. And Lucas still hasn't asked me."

"Is there someone else you can go with? Like girls from the team? Or maybe you don't have to go?"

She scoffs and makes her way back into the dressing room. Her voice is muffled as she audibly struggles to unzip the dress. "You're out of your mind. That's not possible, but thanks for the advice, Savannah."

I cross the room and lean against the wall near her door. "I don't understand why it's so important for you to go to the dance."

"Of course you wouldn't!" She hisses through the door. A moment later, the door swings open and Abby huffs as she throws the dress on the discard rack. "It's just a part of high school, okay? You would understand why these things actually matter if you tried to be a part of everything. But you don't." She starts searching through another heap of shimmering dresses.

I hate the tone of her voice. She's the one who doesn't understand that what she's asking of me is not that easy. Every time I try to explain, this is the result: rejection, blame, failure. I twist my necklace until it bites at the sensitive skin of my neck. I want to keep twisting until I can't breathe.

I clear my throat and avert my eyes from the overwhelming brightness. "I didn't want to come in the first place."

She flips her hair as she turns to me, eyes narrowed. "Yeah, well, you never want to do anything."

I let my necklace go and it thuds against my chest. Every inch of my body burns. Maybe I'm angry or maybe I'm going to cry – I can't really tell. I should just tell Abby the truth: that I want to be interested in dress shopping, I want to be able to go to the school cafeteria and laugh, I want to finally have my first kiss. I have a whole bucket list that I keep folded in the back of my journal. But then I notice how her eyes are fastened to a pile of bargain dresses and I know nothing I say will ever truly matter. My lips meld together as I sacrifice my own sanity and sit back down in the pink, feathered chair.

"When are Bailey and Jacklyn going to get here?" It comes out as a whisper and I have to swallow a few times to soothe my dry throat.

"Soon!" She replies, pulling a layered peach dress from the pile. She holds it against her with a wide smile. Turning to me, she cocks an eyebrow. "What about this one?" By the genuine curiosity in her voice, I know she's forgotten the past few moments.

I trace the modest, silver lace neckline and the slit up the left leg that reaches mid-thigh. The spaghetti straps are also silver and I imagine Abby's hair pinned up with diamond barrettes. "It's beautiful, Abby. Truly."

She shrieks and nearly trips over her own feet as she races back to the dressing room. I can feel her excitement run over my skin and through my veins. But the thin chain continues to pulse and tighten around my neck until all the shades of pink around me blur.

* * *

Two hours and five stores later, everyone is ready for the dance except me. Abby bought the peach dress, along with silver pumps, a diamond clutch, and even set up a hair appointment for the morning of the dance. Bailey fell in love with a burgundy floor length strapless that had tiny diamonds stitched into the midsection. She already had nude heels so she picked up a simple, black purse. Since Jacklyn wasn't going to the dance, she was in charge of helping me pick out a "life altering gown," as she liked to say.

But, true to my unsociable nature, I said no to every dress without even sparing a glance. There was a small part of me that truly wanted to go to the dance but all the effort that went into the preparation was too much; I started getting a headache about thirty minutes in.

"Starbucks break, please?" Begs Abby, readjusting her bags so that she can huddle up to Jacklyn. She blinks and gives her best puppy dog eye impression, a common trope of hers, but the lengthened eyelashes and glittery eyeshadow ruin the effect.

Jacklyn relents anyway. "Fine, but I swear," she points a finger at the numerous bags hanging from Abby's forearm. "You're only getting one drink. You've spent enough. Mom is going to have both our asses if we need to ask for more allowance this month."

Abby smirks, "What about a snack? You know I love my coffee cake." She attempts to rub her belly.

I literally inhale my caramel frappe and blueberry muffin, the mixed flavors sending chills down my spine. It's not the most nutritious meal but it's the first real food I've had in two days. I spread out on a bench and rest my aching feet, thankful for the reprieve.

"I almost forgot!" Bailey plops down beside me as Abby releases her bags in a tsunami of silver and lace. "Apparently,

John is hosting a party next weekend. No parents and alcohol is free."

Abby rubs her hands together, the familiar glint of mischief present in her eyes. "So you're telling me, we get to go to a famous Lutz party and then the spring fling all in the matter of three weeks?"

Jacklyn sips from her cup, her nude lipstick staining the edge. "Just because you're invited doesn't mean you can drink."

Bailey dips a finger into my whip cream, sucks it off, and then starts digging through her bags. "I don't plan to drink anyway. But there is something else..." She pulls out a red two-piece bathing suit and holds it up to her chest. "It's a pool party."

There is a pause as they all try their best not to look at me, faces blank but minds racing. I know they're thinking I'm going to ruin the party or somehow embarrass them. But they don't say that. Instead, Abby throws her coffee cake in the trash.

"No sweets for me. I am now on a cleanse." She proceeds to inspect her hips and midsection, fingers scavenging for invisible imperfections. "I need to try on my bikini. But what if it doesn't fit? Ugh, shopping for bathing suits is the absolute worst!"

"You have like four bikinis, Abby. I'm sure you'll fit into one of them." Jacklyn snaps her head to Bailey. "By the way, when did you buy that?"

Bailey giggles, throwing away both her trash and mine. "I'm good at sneaking away, apparently."

Abby rolls her eyes, "That doesn't matter! What matters is –" She pauses and places her fists on her hips. "The next few weeks are going to be fantastic. Be prepared to take on the world, ladies."

Their voices thin and the light from the windows fade. I don't fight the pull and throw myself into the abyss, basking in the silence of emptiness. Somewhere in the dark, I see a silhouette. He seems to light up from within, engulfing the space around him. His name clings to the tip of my tongue but I won't call out to him. I won't ruin this: the first time I've seen light in the dark.

* * *

I take a deep breath and step forward until I'm at the edge. Water ripples from the center of the lake and gently heaves against the muddy banks. The floating lily pads gently urge me in but when I see my shimmering reflection, the bile rises.

My heart claws its way up my throat and I press my palm to my mouth. I stare at the sun and roll my shoulders, hoping to release the building pressure in my bones.

I look down at the smooth surface and feel a scream push its way past my lips.

There is a little girl floating in the water. Her brunette pigtails break free of their ribbon ties and curls spread out in every direction. She is wearing a bright, blue dress with white polka dots and it balloons around her as she floats to the surface. Her face emerges and again, I let loose a scream that echoes through the trees around me.

I fall to my hands and knees and instantly feel the stinging sensation. My palms burn as rocks attack my skin.

I stare back at myself, noticing the wide eyes and red cheeks. I don't remember myself as a child and there aren't many pictures at my house, but I know that this little girl is me.

She stares back at me, her tiny arms and legs flailing to keep her afloat. She opens her mouth, but I can't pinpoint the exact vowels and consonants. Her hand reaches for mine and just as I'm about to grab it, she is yanked back down.

A white light flashes before my eyes and suddenly, millions of agonizing freeze frames are presented to me. They are bright and rapid and endless.

I have to lie flat on my stomach and hold my head to stop the assault.

Inhale, Exhale. Inhale, Exhale.

My heart becomes steady and I risk a glance at the water.

Tiny bubbles come to the surface and I'm tempted to jump in and risk my life to save another. And I would. If the little girl was real. But the water is undisturbed and that child, although not exactly dead, is gone.

I skim my hands along the water's top and flinch back. I ignore the buzzing in my ears as a white tennis shoe with blue laces floats to the surface.

I can only turn my head to the side and puke.

The Secrets of Her Universe

Aryn

"I found her."

I burrow my face into the embrace of the pillow, trying to ignore Corey's presence as he stands in my doorway. He slowly sits on the end of the bed, moving closer and closer to me until he's right by my ear.

"Wake up. I found your lost girl." His breath is warm and moist.

It only takes me a few seconds to register what he said. I bolt upright in bed, the sheets deciding to stay behind, and my forehead greets Corey's nose. Dust particles float before my eyes as they rattle in their sockets and sunbeams slip in through my sheer curtains.

Corey is large and luminescent when I peek at him, mouth eager and well-oiled. His teeth create craters in his lips and his fingers twist around themselves.

I exhale and lean against my bedpost. "Okay, fill me in."

He literally squeals and crawls in front of me so we are face-to-face. "So I have this friend in Calculus with me, a senior.

74

Her name is Jacklyn Smith. I didn't realize at the time that she was sitting with your mystery girl!"

He takes a deep breath and I feel his eagerness in my chest. It's like he injected sugar into his veins and I'm feeding off his high.

"Okay, Jacklyn Smith. Senior. Got it. Continue."

He rubs his palms up and down his face a few times. "Your lost girl and the mysterious neighbor…" He starts banging on the bed. "Drum roll please!"

Despite myself, I lean forward. His antics are annoying – I don't know why he can't just get to the point – but the building tension has nothing to do with his delay.

"Savannah Mitchell. She's a little reserved but quite feisty, apparently. Jacklyn is a childhood friend."

Savannah.

I clench my fist, sparks consuming the bits of me I no longer need. Her name slips between each tooth and hides itself beneath my tongue. I can taste blueberries. I can smell mud.

"Is that all she told you?"

"Yeah, sorry. She didn't feel comfortable giving out information about Savannah. She seems very protective." He hides his mouth behind his hand. "But she did tell me that Savannah isn't dating anyone."

"Why did she mention that?"

He shrugs, holding his hands up as if in defense. "I may or may not have asked. Anyway, I know it's not a lot of information but at least you know her name." He wags his finger. "Just don't go stalking her! Jacklyn already thinks you like her."

I choke on my tongue. "Why the hell does she think that? I barely know her!"

He stares at me, lips set in a straight line. "Uh, maybe because you were asking around? And because you couldn't stop thinking or talking about her!"

I flip him off. "I had no intention of looking for her. You're the one who asked around!"

"You could've stopped me! A bystander is still a perpetrator!"

I force myself out of bed and flex my stubborn muscles. "My curiosity got the best of me." Going across the hall, I rush to brush my teeth so I can get dressed. "I just wanted to know her name and honestly," I stick my head through the doorframe to look at Corey. He's jumping on my bed. "It fits her so well for some reason. But how come neither of us recognized her? Especially if you're friends with her friend."

He shrugs and plops down on the bed. "Jacklyn didn't clarify, but it seems like Savannah misses a lot of school."

I nod, furrowing my brows. Does her missing school have anything to do with her sleeping in the woods?

"I hope you see her again. I really do." He lies on his stomach and props his head up on his fists, watching me as I come back into the room and pull out clean boxers, a plain grey tee, and jeans.

"Close your eyes." He does as I say but I know he peeks.

"Your ass is marvelous, by the way." He winks and wiggles his fingers at me. "But like I was saying, I hope you see her and I think I know a perfect opportunity."

I glance at him, knowing fully well I shouldn't play his games. But I relent because the chance to see Savannah again is too good to give up. I motion for him to continue, settling back against my dresser in preparation for whatever mad plan he has.

"Well, you know how John is having that pool party next

weekend?"

I nod and walk over to my window.

"Jacklyn said that they're all going. Well, hmm…" I turn to see him rubbing his chin. "She seemed hesitant when I asked if Savannah was going but I'm sure she'll be there! Do you know what that means?"

I shrug and turn back to the window, trying to spot her and the blue gemstone through the dense foliage.

"You can dance with the girl of your dreams, dude!"

A chuckle bursts through my lips on its own accord. I plop down on the bed beside him and pick at a loose thread on my shirt. "What makes you think she'd dance with me or even talk to me?"

He holds up his index finger. "One: you're extremely attractive." He flips up another finger and sends me a wink. "Two: it seems like you guys have a connection."

I grip the sheets. "I was just a dream to her."

"Why do you say that?"

My ribs contain the dying embers of that day, tiny bursts of blue confusion and fist-clenching nightmares. It is simmering out and my head spins at the thought of it disappearing completely.

"Her eyes…" I unclench my fists and spread my fingers out in front of me. "She wasn't really there, Corey. But I can't figure out where she went." I force myself to look at him instead of out the window. "Or if she ever came back."

"If she left and she's lost, we'll find her. Don't worry." He squeezes my shoulder, a wide smile aimed in my direction. "But let's not discuss 'what if,' okay? I need to buy new trunks so it's time to go shopping!"

"Thanks for the offer but I'll stay here." I slide back under my covers.

Corey punches me in the gut and pulls me from the bed. I attempt to cling to the neatly tucked-in sheets but only end up pulling one corner out.

"Corey! I don't want to go to the mall!"

In normal situations, I wouldn't even consider resorting to pouting and whining to get my way. But I loathe going to the mall: it's always congested with giggling girls, overly confident guys, and misbehaved children. So I give Corey my best pout.

"You look ridiculous," he scolds and continues to drag me through the house. "Don't you also need new trunks?"

I scoff and throw him my keys. "I never said I was going to go swimming. And you're driving because I will crash the car before we make it there."

I try my best to curl up in the passenger seat as he turns the key, hoping to evoke whatever compassion he has. But he simply rolls his eyes and pulls out of the driveway.

I cross my arms. "You're heartless."

"And you're a little bitch. Your point?"

I lean back in the seat and stare at the vibrant green trees and pops of red and white blossoms whizzing by. It reminds me of Christmas tinsel or inaudible fireworks.

"Why won't you go swimming, by the way?"

"Why should I?"

He slaps my arm a few times and then gives me a pointed look, as if he shouldn't always have to spell things out for me. Then again, his train of thought veers to places uninhabited by me. "You can see Savannah in a bikini!"

I realize the skin on my face is basically melting off, so I lean my forehead against the cool window. The heat spreads to my ears and neck and I have the urge to rip off all my clothes.

"Oh my god, are you blushing?"

I turn my face into the leather seats. "No, don't be ridiculous."

He reaches over to pinch my cheek. "You're just too adorable!"

I push his hand away and angle my body away from him. "Just focus on driving. Don't wreck my car or I'll murder you in your sleep."

* * *

There are cars crammed haphazardly in between the fading, white lines. People weave between the metallic glint of Hondas and SUVs. I tilt my face toward the floor in a failed attempt to avoid the harsh glare of the sun; the rays come at me from every angle.

The minute we step out of the car I'm drowning in my own perspiration. I pull my shirt away from my body and wipe the accumulating sweat from my neck and brow on Corey's bare arm.

He screeches and pushes me into a dark grey mini cooper. "You're disgusting!" He yells, frantically rubbing his arms. Then he starts running as the Mini Cooper's alarm goes off, shrieks from the abused metal making me sweat for an entirely different reason than the sudden heat wave.

Corey is curled into a ball on the ground when I reach him, his face red from laughter. A mother walks by, holding her child close and glaring at us. I recognize a few guys from school and nod in their direction.

When Corey is finally done straining his lungs and ribs, he stands up and brushes off the tiny particles of dirt, germs, and dead skin cells. I wrap my forearm around his throat and drag him into the cool recess.

The cold is like a hush, soothing my bubbling skin like fingers dipped in water and tongues caressed by iced cubes. It should be quiet because people willingly and silently give up their souls here. But they still find ways to make noise, to make pointless conversation.

"Whoa," Corey grips my arm. "It's a fucking madhouse in here."

I shake him free and stuff my hands in my pockets. "Let's just get your shit and leave. I don't want to be here all day."

Rolling his eyes, he leads me through a crowd of elderly women dressed in paisley dresses, who are complaining about the meaty smell of the food court. When we pass by them, I hear their gasp of outrage at the "rude behavior of young people." I have to bite my lip to keep from laughing.

Corey is on his phone, speaking softly into the receiver. He meets my glance, smirks, and then quickly looks away. I shove my hands deeper into my pockets, following him as he ventures toward the food court.

"Dude, if you're going to eat, please don't take an hour like you usually do."

Corey holds up his index finger and mumbles something into the phone. Then he turns to me with a smile made of teeth. "We're meeting some friends. Do you remember where Starbucks is?"

"Friends? We don't have any other friends!"

"Speak for yourself. Now let's go."

I throw my head back, maybe to release a war cry or in an attempt to snap my neck. Either way, he still leads me to the tiny shop filled to the brim with ventis and misspelled names and lines that never end. There are wooden benches outside and we head toward one with four girls.

At first, I'm just Corey's puppy, following on his heels like he has my chew toy. But when I see who's on the bench, I shudder to a stop.

Before I knew her name, I had the feeling she was simply a ghost. An entity that couldn't be tied to this place. But she showed herself to me and I held on, gripped her fingers and kept her planted here because I was curious. I was fascinated.

Now I know she is not a ghost because I see her sitting there. Corey sees her sitting there. But Corey doesn't see her like I do. He doesn't understand why, even though she's just a few feet from us, she is out of our reach.

Her hair is no longer in a single braid but falls in tight curls around her shoulders, not a halo but a shield. Her head is tilted up, eyes focused on something outside the skylight. I follow her line of vision, but I only see the blue sky and blaring sun.

She's wearing a white layered dress, the bodice hugging her torso and flaring at her hips. Her feet are encased in black flats with ribbons that wrap around her ankle. She is swinging her legs back and forth and each time she moves them back, her muscles tighten beneath the fabric.

The three girls surrounding her are engrossed in conversation, seemingly oblivious to Savannah's presence.

"Did you set this up?" I don't mean to sound breathless, but she has already knocked me down and set me ablaze twice. Corey takes my panting for anger and recoils, glancing between me and the bench.

"Don't be mad," he pleads, clasping his hands together in a silent prayer.

I'm far from angry but dangerously unprepared. My legs quiver but I zig zag behind Corey anyway. The girls abruptly drop the ends of their sentences and stare. The girl I assume to be Jacklyn wraps an arm around Corey's waist and they exchange chaste kisses, making dramatic sound effects and all.

"This is Aryn," Corey forces me to shake their hands and I try my best to stamp their names into my memory. When I turn to Savannah, her eyes are still diverted upward. I slide my hand back into my pocket.

The girl closest to Savannah, Bailey, shakes her auburn hair and gently taps Savannah's shoulder. She twitches but remains focused on the skylight.

"I'm sorry about her," This is Abby, who simultaneously smells of grass and sugar. She places her hand on Savannah's head, like one would do to console a toddler. "She does this a lot. Kind of just blanks out." A shrug and the issue is dismissed.

"But is she okay?" I clear my throat and try my best to match gazes with Bailey, who stands closest to Savannah. I notice that her hand keeps travelling to Savannah's shoulder every other minute. As if to make sure she hasn't disappeared.

Bailey narrows her eyes at me. "She's fine." I can't tell if she's angry, threatened, or just curious. She turns back to the others.

Abby squeals with excitement as they start discussing the pool party, but this moment is the only thing that matters.

I don't know how I summon the courage but the next thing I know, I'm thigh to thigh with her. Her skin glistens like freshly poured caramel and she still smells like soil and wild blueberries. I tap her elbow with mine and the reaction is instant but unexpected.

She turns to me with dead eyes, the dim light reflecting my image in shimmering waves. She looks right through me, into another plane or dimension. I want to be there, too. I want to dive into the pools of light in her eyes and travel to where she is.

She has rendered me invisible and mute, the space around her devoid of skin and lips and hearts. But I don't know how her mind fills that empty space. Can she only see shadows? Is she surrounded by night, even when the sun dominates the sky? Or does she somehow shroud herself in pure light?

My throat burns with questions, but I force them to remain and I taste acid. Her departure is not a concern, but the catalyst is.

I stand, skin not yet ready to leave hers. I stare Corey down until he cannot see anyone else but me. As we say the customary goodbyes, I allow myself one more glance.

She stares back at me, a tiny crease in her otherwise symmetrical eyebrows. A smile edges its way into the corner of her mouth but the fire in my chest has rekindled full force so I turn away.

Again, I lie my palm on my chest and beg the fire to recede.

"You okay, man?" Corey pokes my cheek. "You're extremely red. How can you be flustered when she didn't even talk to you?" He looks back over his shoulder. "I have to admit, she's a cutie."

I hold up a finger. "Let's not talk about it." I stuff my balled fists in my pockets.

Even when we're done shopping, I can still feel her skin against my elbow and see her lips cradling secrets only she knows.

Ghost

Savannah

"I feel like you've grown so much."

My mother's tongue is stained with what looks to be red Kool-Aid and her lips smack together as words fall to the floor. I lean forward to catch them, but I don't even understand her language. She's just making sounds.

"You've only been gone a month."

She opens a few cabinets. "It feels like I've been gone longer. It looks like it, too, since there's nothing in here except for instant noodles."

My stomach churns. "I eat out with the girls."

"Do they ever come over? You shouldn't be in this house alone all the time."

Apparently, I didn't purge my body of the entire blueberry muffin because remnants are slowly climbing up my throat. I gather saliva in my cheeks and swallow, but the taste still lingers on my tongue. "Why don't you stay then? Longer than usual, I mean."

A sigh erupts from her throat and clings to her thick lipstick.

"You know how time-consuming digs are. I can't just leave the excavation sites in the hands of my crew."

I cup my ears, a dull buzzing sound muffling her words. "What about dad?"

She shakes her head and the buzzing crescendos until the house's skeleton shakes. Cracks spider across the windows and the floor splits beneath my feet. I grip the edge of my chair, bones aching against the pressure. Her mouth keeps moving and the dismantling of this house, of the people who should be living here, continues.

"Nothing will change if you sell the house and we move, will it? I still won't be living in a home."

She sighs, "Savannah, we still don't even know if we're selling the house. It was more of an idea, rather than a plan."

"An idea you didn't think to discuss with me. Like I'm not here alone all the time."

My mother places two steaming mugs of coffee on the quivering table but the dark liquid does not ripple. The steam rises and tumbles in the stale air, flicking at the tip of my nose. The bitter smell makes the vomit resurface.

It won't stop. It never stops: the splintering, the quarantine, the darkness. My breath falters in my chest when I move too fast and runs rampant when everything is still.

How often do I stand in one spot because there is nowhere else for me to go?

Why is there darkness, even when all the lights are on?

I remember lying in a patch of sun when I visited him once, stretching out my sore limbs. Popping joints and pulling muscles like banana taffy. My skin tingled but I couldn't tell if it was from the heat or the medication. I closed my eyes and the sun still managed to climb beneath my eyelids, throwing golden dots everywhere. It was beautiful.

Until it suddenly wasn't. Until the hair on my arms rose and I saw rays of light melding into the tree bark and digging graves into the soil. But there was a bubble around me that the sun could not penetrate. My fingers tried to grasp the thin gleams. My tongue tried to lap up the heat. But there was tar biting at my fingers and clogging my lungs. Every day after that, the sun struggled to rise for me.

When the warmth faded, it took with it my parents' smiles. It took unfiltered laughter and the ease of an embrace. It was then that my mother took her pain and neatly tucked it away into suitcases which she flew with across the oceans. My father, on the other hand, chased his pain with various tinted bottles and eventually he, too, packed away the hurt and fled. It's been months since I last saw him, years since we last actually spoke. Maybe he went looking for a place where the sun still shone.

And now my mother is back in this cold place. She is still talking but the house has settled and the windows have healed. She drinks her coffee black, miniscule grounds dancing in her mouth and sticking to her bright lips.

The steam rises. I try to swallow it. The steam rises. I want to feel that warmth.

The tip of my pinky goes in, burns, and seeks refuge in my mouth. A ground steals space on my tongue. I bury two spoonfuls of sugar and vanilla creamer into the mug, swirling and creating a tidal wave that pushes the creamy liquid over the edge. It slowly spreads, gathering at the base and then infecting the entire table. It seeps into the wood and latches onto my mother's papers. She scrambles, fingers hurriedly trying to rescue sodden maps and instructions. She is eager to rescue her work but not her own daughter.

I lift the mug to my lips, feel the steam rising, and use the coffee to chase the bile. I finger the rejected grounds in my cup as the caffeine stimulates my nerves. My mother cleans up my mess, her mess. I feel it clawing its way back up, but I do not push it back down this time. I will the darkness to come, to shroud me in nothingness, but it offers no solace.

There is blueberry muffin everywhere.

* * *

There are two bodies here, with twitching muscles and inflating lungs. Shiny teeth and taut skin.

But the house is still empty. Still waiting for warm hands and beating hearts. I am against the walls, in the shadows, waiting for the same thing. I have been waiting for such a long time.

My mother keeps flashing bright smiles at me in between phone conversations and hurried data reports. I stare at the peeling, blue nail polish on my bitten-down fingers and try to ignore the sound of backspaces. It's harder to ignore the pride in her voice as she describes a vase found in ruins on a forgotten island.

How she loves forgotten and dirt-covered things.

How she loves to forget everything else.

"How long will you be here?" My voice echoes.

She holds up two fingers. Her time is always numbered in days. Two days with her teenage daughter, 30 days in consecrated caves and abandoned villages, 365 days finding missing pieces of lost civilizations.

"I'm assuming you haven't spoken to dad lately?"

She points to the phone tightly glued to her ear and turns

in her seat. The coffee pot starts brewing another six cups of energy. The clock starts slowing down. My head is spinning.

"I'm going on a walk."

No response. I cover my mouth as the dark roast scent fills the air, wiggle my toes into faded sandals and sprint out the front door. My body tips to the side, legs wobbly and arms stiff. I collide with outstretched branches whose bony fingers test the cushion of my skin. Clumps of weeds latch onto my toes and beg me to stay.

My feet move on their own accord, avoiding sinkholes but greeting piles of dry soil. I feel the grains between my toes and under my nails. I can smell vibrant blooms and unpolluted water. Water that glistens unscathed beneath the sun's probing fingers. Water that reflects back a carbon-copy image. Water that holds tiny shoes and silk ribbons. Water that I cannot touch.

I sit away from the very edge, where it's still damp and mossy. The mud seeps into the back of my shorts. I slip off my sandals and submerge my toes into the gooey mound until they are completely covered. I grab fistfuls of the mud, letting it fall from my fingers in globs.

I lean back and focus on the migrating clouds. There should be shapes, like bunnies and flowers and mythical creatures. But there are only clouds pulled apart like yarn and stretched into wispy threads. The sun hides behind these pools of thread, a coward in its own palace. It quivers, sending light in small strips across the lake. I can almost feel the licks of heat. Almost.

"Savannah?"

My heart pushes against my chest and I have to fill my lungs with shaky gulps of air before I can follow the voice. I tip my head back, the mud squishing, and see a boy hanging upside down. He has serious bedhead, with thin, pale lips, and a crooked, upturned nose – or downturned at this angle. His shoulders are broad and I trace the lean expanse of his torso.

"Ah, my mysterious neighbor has returned."

Aryn frowns and takes a step closer. "Are you alright?"

I look back to the sky and resume my search for unicorns and daisies. "Uh, yes. Why wouldn't I be?"

"Well... why are you lying in mud?"

"It's comfortable. The mud is cool."

"But you're going to get all dirty." He peers into my face, eyebrows drawn.

"So?" I pivot my head to the right, but he follows suit. I lean to the left. "Do you mind? You're in my way."

He stands beside me and I can feel his body heat. My fingers twitch.

"What are you looking at?"

I point up, fingers covered in brown goo. Some of it falls onto my chest and I rub it in, the grainy texture therapeutic. "The clouds. Trying to find something interesting in them but I can't."

Aryn grunts, lowering himself onto his back beside me. My muscles clench, knees subconsciously trying to curl into my chest. He is too close. So close that my skin starts to itch and I wrap my arms around my stomach to keep from scratching.

"I see a bird."

I click my tongue and try to follow his line of vision. "I don't see anything."

He grabs my wrist, fingers enveloped in watered-down soil. He uncurls my index finger, which I don't remember forming into a fist, and points to a gray pile of thread. I trace the outline and when I see the shape of a beak, my throat emits a sound born from both pleasure and shock.

"It really is a bird!"

I turn to him and snatch my hand away when I'm confronted by eyes shaped like almonds. I sit up, pulling my feet out of the mud and slamming my legs into my chest. My fingers instinctively tie themselves into knots, but there is so much energy pulsing through them.

"I can't believe this is the first time I've seen something in the clouds. I look almost every day I'm out here."

He pops up beside me. Mud slowly crawls down his back. "You come out here a lot, right?"

I nod, leaning forward to keep pressure on my bubbling stomach.

"I only come out here to run. Usually before school."

"It's nice out here in the morning. The soil is still soft, and the grass is covered in dew." I stretch my arms out and take a deep breath. "The air somehow smells... cleaner."

He chuckles. "Yeah, it is. I plug in my headphones and just follow the trail. Relieves any stress."

"You don't really need music." I shake my feet in an effort to get rid of some mud and slip my sandals on. There is an embarrassingly loud squishing sound when I stand up.

He, again, follows my lead. "It's too quiet out here."

"Isn't the silence loud enough?"

Aryn pauses and briefly glances around. "What do you mean?"

"If you're out here long enough, you begin to hear all the smallest sounds the trees and animals make. It can be quite creepy. Almost like your mind is playing tricks on you."

He tilts his head, eyes roaming the scenery before landing on me. "Okay, yeah, of course there are the sounds of nature.

But those sounds don't measure up to listening to music."

I stand on tiptoe so I can whisper in his ear, too afraid to disturb the other voices speaking around me. "Close your eyes and just listen." He stares at me for a moment too long. But then he nods, eyelids slowly shutting. I go back onto my soles but remain close so I can feel the heat from his skin. I can't help but trace the crooked line of his nose and the stubble on his chin.

I pinch my forearm and take a step back. "Out here, the sound isn't manufactured. The wind moves on its own accord and always whispers secrets to the trees. Do you hear them giggling?"

He tilts his head to the side, eyebrows furrowing in concentration. I can see his eyes darting left and right under his eyelids, eager to catch any sound.

"What about the leaves? Can you hear them whirling like tiny helicopters as they fall to the ground?" I watch him turn in a circle and take a few steps toward a tree. But he doesn't say anything.

I start to stomp on twigs as I walk squares around him. The wind is spreading gossip now and the trees chortle with unsuppressed glee. The leaves are diving from the highest branch and taking their last breathes in the cold mud. The water laps against the bank where weeds grow, again and again. Every sound crescendos with fervor yet he remains planted to one spot, head titled and eyes searching beneath closed lids.

I throw my hands in the air and search the sky again for the bird-shaped cloud. "You don't hear anything, right?"

"No, I do." My eyes snap to his face and his eyes are hooded. He takes a step toward me and my limbs pulse and tremble. "I probably can't hear everything you can, but I hear the wind and the leaves shaking."

"You think I'm crazy." I stare up at the clouds, desperately seeking a patch of sunlight.

"Not at all. My inability to hear or see more than what's right in front of me in no way diminishes how you perceive the world. And being alone with one's own thoughts, being surrounded by that fake silence, is actually quite... intrusive." One corner of his mouth tips up and my palms start to sweat. His sneakers squelch has he walks through the thin mud until he's directly in front of me. "But if the silence is too much for you, why are you always out here?"

"I have my reasons." A gust of wind picks up stranded leaves and throws them carelessly into the water. Silence blinds me and knocks me down no matter where I am. The only thing that changes is what causes it: I can't control the mind-numbing quiet that saturates the walls of my house. But I can surround myself with shadows that attempt to speak but are used to being ignored. That is the silence I can swallow without spitting it back out.

"Can I guess?"

I stare into his glistening eyes that remind me of rich chocolate. His curiosity makes my skin itch and my fingers yearn to latch onto him. I shouldn't speak but he seems so eager to hear me, so I tip my chin into my chest and wait.

He grins and while he starts circling me, I can't help but stare at his mouth again. The shape it makes seems so familiar to me, like I have seen it over and over in a dream.

"Hmm..." He peers into my face every few seconds. When he does, I can feel his breath on my lips. "You have younger siblings who always make too much noise and invade your privacy, so you come out here to bask in nature's glory?"

"Only child."

His grin briefly disappears, and he snaps his fingers. He stands toe-to-toe with me but inspects our surroundings. "You have a heavy workload and get stressed easily. This amazing scenery refreshes you?"

I roll my eyes. "High school is obviously shitty. That's a universal fact." I purse my lips. "But I guess you're on the right track."

Aryn rubs his hands together and again, he lifts one corner of his mouth. It almost resembles a twitch. It makes my chest concave. "I'm so good at this!" He boasts and leans in once again. He just stares at me, eyes roaming from my forehead to my chin.

It hurts to breathe.

Eventually, his mouth straightens. He doesn't look away for even a second. Although his voice is merely a whisper, it resounds in my ear. "You're lonely."

I blink and step back. "What?"

He follows me, lips still set in a straight line. "I don't know why and I won't ask or try guessing. But you're lonely."

I scoff and push against his chest. "I have plenty of friends, thank you very much."

He laughs, but it doesn't sound humorous at all. He shakes his head and dark locks fall into his eyes. "You don't have to be alone to feel lonely."

I cross my arms over my chest. "You shouldn't just assume things."

He shakes his head again and stares unflinchingly into my eyes. I swallow. "I'm not assuming anything. I knew it the moment we first met."

"Knew that I was lonely?"

He finally takes a step back and smiles. Once again I feel as if I've been here before, standing in front of this boy. If he has the same feeling he doesn't let it show. "I knew something was wrong. No one sleeps out in the wilderness just because."

"This is hardly the wilderness, and people go camping all the time."

His mouth is at my ear in an instant. "But we both know you weren't camping."

The heat from his mouth makes me shiver. I push at his chest again. "Why are you so curious? Do you probe people with questions like these all the time?"

"Nope! Just you." His grin seems to swallow everything around us.

I open my mouth but only a sigh escapes. In the absence of his voice, I notice that it's too quiet. The wind has stopped whispering. My nails find their way into the muscles of my upper arm; they are ruthless.

There is a stingy sensation. One that I'm used to. And it feels so much better than the pain in my chest he's causing.

"Why don't you like the quiet out here?"

He pauses, tilting his head as if to search for sounds. "You're changing the subject."

"And you're avoiding the question." I feel the muscles in my jaw twitch.

His grin still hasn't disappeared. "Well... I'm always so used to my sister running around the house screaming or laughing. Or my best friend talking my ear off, so I don't handle the silence very well."

There is blood welling up under my fingernails. "That makes sense."

"Does it?"

I nod but can't look at him. How can he be so open with me when he doesn't even know me? "Silence isn't always a reprieve." I look up this time and his eyes burn holes into my skin. "Sometimes your mind turns against you."

"Does your mind turn against you?" Aryn invades my bubble with his warmth and pries my fingers away from my now red skin. He runs his palms down my upper arms, mixing mud with blood.

The wind would be a great excuse right now because my body can't stop trembling, yet my skin is set ablaze. I pull away from him.

"I think the mud is starting to harden. I should probably go wash up."

He chuckles, picking off a clump of mud from his shirt. "You're really good at avoiding questions. You'll have to teach me your ways."

I just shake my head because the sight of his wide smile and mud-covered body causes rapid flashes of light to go off behind my eyes. Just like that day in my father's office. It's like my mind desperately wants me to remember something, remember *him,* but it hurts when I try.

Another chuckle, effortlessly pouring out from his gut and caressing my skin. My jaw is sore.

"Can I walk you home?"

I can't control the way my fingers curl into fists or the way my chest tightens. As a precaution, I tuck my elbows into my side and grip my necklace like the life preserver is it.

I am moving. Away. Back to the house with no heart and eager hands.

"Savannah? Why are your eyes closed?" My name rolls off his tongue with such precision that my throat dries up. My heart is flailing inside my chest. I feel heat rising from the pit of my stomach.

"I'm sorry. I just…" Deep breath. "Need to go."

"Open your eyes, Savannah." He cups my face for just a moment. But one moment is all it takes for me to let his heat sink in. One moment for the words to get stuck in my throat and the tears to mark acid trails down my cheeks.

Aryn steps back, releasing my scorching face and offering me his hand. It is covered in watery soil and specks of my blood. He doesn't try to dry my tears or ask any questions. I don't have the answers even if he did. "Lead the way."

My mind screams in protest as I slide my palm over his. I have to swallow bile back down. But I grip his fingers despite the urge to flee and hide. I grip his fingers and take him home.

Two steps and I'm trembling. Six and he has to wrap his arm around my waist, lifting me up in fear of being dragged down. Thirty and I'm numb.

Do you know what's worse than a house with hidden skeletons and vengeful ghosts?

A house that's haunted by me.

Mud has a Secret

Aryn

Her blood got everywhere.

There wasn't even that much, just tiny half-moon indents shedding whatever rages inside her. But where there is mud there is red. On my palms, under my nails, tiny splashes on my cotton tee. Her nails chewed her skin in such a slow, purposeful manner that I could tell she's done it before. Her arms must be littered with scabbed-over crescents.

She stumbles, with limbs of a newborn, and I pull her tightly into me until her hip bone digs into my thigh. Her arms wrap around her chest and her shoulders quiver slightly; little jerks propel her bare skin into my armpit.

I want to go back. Back to the forest and the silence. Before I let my tongue keep spitting out words. Before she receded into herself once again and left me alone, covered in mud.

"We're here." Her voice is surprisingly even – like I'm not basically carrying her blood and mud-covered body home – that it takes me a few moments to process what she said.

Her house resembles mine in architecture: pillars, large

mahogany door, too many windows and a huge chimney Santa would love to climb down. But her house is so stark white it's blinding. I almost wish we could throw mud at all the window panes just to add color.

"Your house is beautiful."

She snorts, disentangling herself from my side to dig her key out from her mud-caked shorts. She smears soil over the solid, white wood and stares at it before turning the key until it clicks. "Mhm, it's… architecturally sound."

A burst of cold air greets me as she opens the door. I can't help but peek inside; there is nothing but white walls and the smell of dust. "You don't like it?"

A laugh crescendos into a cough. "Well to be quite honest, it's too large for my taste. Everything echoes." She turns to face me, leaning against the doorframe.

"Ah, I see. Does it feel like you're in a horror movie?" For some reason, I wiggle my eyebrows. And immediately regret it.

"Majority of the time." Her eyes snap to focus on something over my shoulder and I almost turn around to see if, somehow, a hooded figure is standing behind me.

"Are you afraid?"

Her eyes meet mine and then roam my entire face before lingering on my mouth. As if she's waiting for me to ask again. "Afraid of what?"

I shrug. "This house? Random noises? Resentful spirits?"

"Oh," Her body straightens, almost falling backward into the house. "Not anymore. I never used to want to sleep because the house was just so empty that I always believed *something* would materialize from all the unoccupied space."

"And now?"

"Those thoughts aren't the reason I can't sleep. I'm not scared of things that go bump in the night. I've learned to love them."

I'm not rattled by the off chance of being murdered tonight. I'm shaken senseless by the fact that Savannah seems to live in an entirely different universe than the rest of us. Who befriends the monsters under their bed instead of seeking help? Who can sleep through nightmares of hands reaching out and latching onto exposed skin?

It's one thing if she has no choice but to live in the shadows, where mayhem and bodiless voices are sure to thrive. It's another thing entirely if she chooses to live there.

I slide my shaky hands into my pockets. "I just can't figure you out."

She grips the doorframe. "No one asked you to. No one asked you to say one word to me."

"I know but when I saw you the other day, I just had to-"

"Had to what?" Her eyes meet mine and there's the trembling from before, like everything she sees makes her bones shake. Or the rage that's inside her, the rage that's also in me, begins to boil again. "Pity the mental case who sleeps in the fucking forest so you can say you've done your charity work for the year? Or did you think it'd be fun trying to diagnose me?"

My hands can't seem to unclench. "No, no... That's not it at all!"

"Then what?" Her hand flies to her mouth, fingers quivering. I can hear her swallow; words, vomit, I don't know.

"I don't know... I just had to talk to you. I have to... I have to know you. But I can't explain it." I know I've already lost her, her body receding into the dust-covered recess of her empty house.

"Do me a favor, okay?" She tilts her head to the side and

narrows her eyes. "When you figure it out, keep it to yourself."

I see white and pull my hands out of my pockets, stretch the bundled muscles out so I can see the brown and red speckled skin. I want to knock on the closed door but what could I possibly say?

And do I even want the door to open again? I may not like what comes out this time.

* * *

"So…" Corey stuffs a handful of Cheetos into his mouth. "What's her secret?" He folds his legs beneath him and turns to me, eyebrows raised.

The hood of my car squeaks as I reposition myself, the metal crying out in agony beneath my weight. "She doesn't have to have this huge secret to explain her slamming the door in my face."

"Hey, I'm just saying. According to what you've told me, she's done some weird shit." He pops his thumb into his mouth and sucks off all the cheese. "There's a high possibility that she's a psychopath, or is in the witness protection program." His shoulders meet his ears.

I hop off the hood. "Everything that comes out of your mouth lately is bullshit. You know that, right?"

He shrugs again and tips the Cheeto bag upside down over his mouth, inhaling any leftover particles. "I'm bored. Like… extremely."

"Everyone has secrets, dude. Just because she doesn't invite me into her house and let me read her diary, doesn't mean she's hiding corpses in her closet."

I don't have to look at him to know he's just rolled his eyes. "Mhm, but only a sociopath would listen to the voices in the walls. I feel like now you're just trying to find excuses."

"Excuses for what?" I try to stare into the sun so I can feel some sort of burn, so I can feel the pain I must.

"Excuses to still be interested. You need to justify everything she does because for some convoluted reason – a reason neither of us can actually pinpoint – you are weirdly infatuated with this girl."

"Excuses aren't needed, Corey. She's interesting."

"She's bizarre."

"Dude, why are you being so judgmental lately?" I turn to him, his fingers still greedily searching the edges of the Cheeto bag. "Everything I say about her is just ammunition for you. Why do you have such an issue with her?"

He sticks his fingers in his mouth once more before crumpling the bag into a tiny ball and throwing it through the driver's side window. "I just don't want you to latch onto another girl to distract yourself, okay?"

"What do you mean?"

He sucks in all the air around him. "When your dad died, you were…" He flings his hands around, hoping to catch the word he's looking for. "You were a shell. You didn't talk, pretty sure you were numb, and my god, were you angry."

I suck my teeth. "Pretty sure that's a logical way for someone to mourn."

"No shit. But then you got with Clara and stopped trying to get better. You let her weasel her way into your life, man. And because of her, I don't believe you ever truly healed."

I slide my hands into my jean pockets so he can't see the fists. "Does anyone truly heal after a loss like that?"

"You still haven't forgiven yourself, is what I mean. It's almost been three years and you're still punishing yourself." He tries to catch my gaze. "The sun can't burn away your guilt, bro."

I blink away tears and try to cool my tingling skin. "What do you suggest I do then? Forgiving yourself isn't as easy as forgiving others."

"Just don't let the mystery of this girl distract you from confronting your demons. With the anniversary coming up... It's about time you came to grips with what happened. Truly."

"It's just... I have a gut feeling." I pause, going back to sit next to him. I uncurl my fists and swallow the delusion that sticks to my tongue. But Corey pries it out of me anyway.

"What gut feeling?"

The hood of the car warms my upper thighs. "This is going to sound so stupid, but I can't shake this feeling. Ever since I saw her that day in the woods, there is a need to see her and know her. I've never felt this way about anyone else and it doesn't make sense. I know that."

He hums, tapping his fingers against the metal. "Do you think it's love at first sight or something?"

I shrug. "I'm not even sure if I believe in love at first sight." But I want to because Savannah is more than just an intriguing stranger. I feel connected to her in a way I cannot define. The possibility of speaking to her, of being under her gaze, makes me breathless and eager and more terrified than I have ever been in my life. But I don't tell Corey this. Instead, I say: "If I lose myself, you have permission to punch me in the face again. Deal?"

He grins, bright orange cheese stuck to his teeth. "On one condition: I can wear brass knuckles this time. Surely that will get my point across much quicker."

Run to Me

Savannah

"Why are you still in bed?"

Bailey's voice is like a bucket of freezing water. I slam my knees deep into my chest and manage to force my swaddled hand out from under the covers to flip her off. That's my warning in case she tries to force me out of bed, but she simply giggles.

"My bed seduced me."

She tugs at the corner of my blanket. "It's 3 o'clock, Savannah. You missed an entire day of school and no one knew where you were. When did you go to sleep last night?"

My foot attempts to hold down the blanket but she rips it away from me. My leg accidently connects with her stomach.

"Ow, what the hell!"

I immediately regret opening my eyes because it feels as if the sun spits on my corneas with acid-laced saliva. "Let's see... I fell asleep around 10 this morning. School was definitely not an option." I stuff my head back under the pillow.

Bailey groans and slaps my exposed thigh. "Well, you can't

just decide not to go to school. Did something happen? Is that why you were up all night?" She pinches my love handles this time and I roll over until my body meets the carpeted floor.

I look at her through my tangled curls, chest heaving. "Why do you assume that me trying to murder you at 3 p.m. needs to have a reason?"

Her eyes expand. "You were trying to kill me?"

I shrug, crawling back onto the bed. "If I told you that, I'd definitely have to kill you."

She stares at me in silence for a moment before taking a seat at the edge of my bed. A deep sigh travels up her throat. "We've been best friends for what feels like forever, so can you please just be honest with me this once?"

I sprawl out on the bed next to her, linking my pinky with hers. This is how I initiate contact. "I just had a very stressful evening."

"Elaborate."

I grip her pinky tighter, the little contact somehow reassuring. "My mom is back. Or was back; I don't know if she is still here. So yeah, that's one stressful thing."

She props herself up on her elbow, eyebrows furrowed. "There's more, I'm guessing."

I avoid her gaze, instead turning onto my back and staring at the ceiling. "Aryn, he... He just pisses me off."

She's quiet, so much so that I'm forced to turn back toward her. She is simply staring at me, a small smile planted on her lips. Her eyes, however, are still furrowed.

"What is that face for?"

"It's been like what, a week? And already something has changed since you've met him. You're..." She points her index finger at me. "More. That's the only way I can think to describe it."

I face her completely now, our faces inches apart. "That makes absolutely no sense."

"His presence is getting under your skin." She touches her nose to mine. "In a good way, like he's somehow gently forcing you out of your comfort zone. Do you understand what I mean? Like even now, look how close I am to you and you're not trying to run away."

I put my hand in front of my face, purposely defying her last statement. "If you mean he's annoying as shit and won't stop prying into my life, then yes."

"What you mean is that he actually listens to you, right?" I nod, pulling my hand to my chest. "That's something the girls and I aren't very good at. We focus too much on making sure you're eating and not trying to... you know."

My pinky leaves hers. "Kill myself?"

A moment of silence. The wind taps against the window panes. "Not trying to sabotage the progress you've made so far. We've become so accustomed to making decisions for you, because for a while you weren't making the right ones." She curls up next to me and throws her arm across my stomach, which grumbles with emptiness. "I'm so sorry that we've treated you like a child who can't tie their own shoes."

"I let you."

"Don't let us. Not anymore. We all know that you have so much fire inside you, so many aspirations that can't be quelled by those pesky mind tricks of yours."

I turn away from her and all the bullshit she's spewing. "Bailey, do you even know what you're saying right now? Pesky mind tricks, really?" I pull out of her embrace and basically run to the window, eager for an external source of heat. "I don't understand why you're saying all of this now. Why you expect me to be a different and better person suddenly, because of this boy. That's not how recovery works."

She follows me, arms immediately wrapping around my frame. Encasing all the bubbling anxiety. Holding me together once again, because for some reason I cannot do that on my own.

"That's not what I meant and you know it. I just want you to be happy. Or to at least enjoy things, like photography. Does it even make you smile anymore?"

I don't know where to look or how to hold my body. "I'm trying."

She forces a laugh out. "Are you really? Because if you were trying, you'd be eating or telling your parents they need to come home."

I try to pull away, but she tightens her grip. I feel trapped beneath her gaze and in this house. "It's not as easy as that. They don't listen. No one listens."

"Make them." She forces me to look at her. "Make everyone finally hear you."

I can only nod against her shoulder, ribs aching from unknowingly holding in breaths.

"We don't have to talk about this right now, but you have to admit that you feel different than before. Whether it's pure annoyance or something more, please admit that you don't just feel numb anymore."

I nod against her again, breathing into her, breathing her in. "I can't explain why…"

"Why what?"

"I want to see him again. That's why I couldn't sleep. I was thinking about him all night and I… I shouldn't have skipped school, but I got queasy when I thought about possibly seeing him."

She runs her hands over my hair and pulls me into a hug, so tight I lose my breath. All she says, in a whisper that sounds like a secret, is: "I'm proud of you."

Proud of what? I'm not exactly sure and I don't have the energy to ask. But it makes me weak in the knees; it makes me forget that my throat hurts from all the words I vomited.

When we separate, I still question whether I can speak truthfully from now on. Just the thought of speaking loud enough to be heard makes my entire body tremble. How can I possibly say what's always been on the tip of my tongue? How will the world react when they realize my voice is rusty and that when I speak, I must also bleed?

Those who are silenced have a lot to say. And those who have silenced us should be terrified when we finally speak.

* * *

Bailey wraps herself in a multitude of blankets, attempting to shield herself from the blood splatter on the TV screen. After the screams subside – a mixture of the fictional victims and Bailey's constant woes –, she leans into me, hands flailing to grab a hold of me through the layers of fabric.

"Is this what makes you happy? People being murdered?"

I dig my shoulder into her ribs. "It is quite hilarious when they get their heads cut off."

Her eyes widen. "How on earth is that funny?"

The screen goes dark as the protagonist hides in a black-outed cellar. "There are rules to surviving a horror movie.

When you hear a strange noise, you definitely don't go investigate or scream "who's there?" because it makes you an easy target."

She gasps. "Are you saying they deserve to be brutally murdered?"

"Well..." I shrug, digging around the popcorn bowl for the lone piece without a kernel. "Stupid actions have consequences. The moral of any horror movie is to make good life choices."

Even in the dark, I can see Bailey roll her eyes. "I honestly can't tell if you're being serious or not." She palms my face and stretches my cheeks until my lips form a smile. "Awh, there you go. Wearing a smile feels good, doesn't it?"

I lean forward until my nose touches her. "I will bite your finger off if you don't stop touching me."

Instantly, she pulls back. "I still have the scar from the last time you bit me, you savage." She tucks her hands back into the safety of the blankets.

Once the movie's credits start rolling, Bailey jumps up and flips on the lights. She takes out the disc and replaces it with *Sing*, clapping her hands together in excitement. "No more murder, only beautiful animation and singing. I'll go make more popcorn!" She wrestles the bowl from my hands and literally skips into the kitchen.

The room is shrouded in light but silence. The wind picks up outside the window, the sun slowly descending and casting shadows on the driveway pavement. A chill sweeps through the house and I must wrap a blanket around myself and bring my knees to my chest in order to stop from shivering.

The microwave beeps and I can smell butter. My stomach grumbles. I hear a light knock, pull the blanket tighter around me and walk into the kitchen. "You okay in here?"

She continues emptying the steaming bag of popcorn into the bowl, not even looking up. "I'm fine, why?" She hands me the bowl and goes to the fridge to take out two iced teas. The knock comes again and she spins around to face me, hands gripping the bottles and eyes devouring her entire face. "Were you expecting company?"

I stare into the living room, racking my brain for any information that may have been knocked loose. "Nope."

Bailey screeches. "Wait! Where the hell are you going?"

I don't pause, feet moving forward even as she tugs on my arm. "Someone's knocking so obviously I'm going to answer the door."

"But I mean…" She whispers against my neck. "What if it's a deranged sociopath with an unquenchable bloodthirst?"

"One can only hope." I hold her at arm's length. "If they are wielding a knife, then run out the back door. Don't try hiding and don't fall. If you fall then you kind of deserve to die." I offer my best sympathetic smile and twist the doorknob.

And there he is, shrouded by the flickering shadows yet still ablaze. His face is hardly recognizable, not because of the impending dark around us, but because his eyes shift back and forth like he's seen a ghost. I'm tempted to look down at myself to see if I'm somehow translucent.

"Hey, Savannah. And Bailey." Aryn throws us a weak smile as he rubs his neck raw. "I don't mean to barge in on you, especially so late." A pause filled by him pressing his lips together. "I just… My mother and sister aren't coming home tonight and my house is a little too empty for comfort."

I can only stare. Swallowing does nothing to lessen the lump in my throat. I am choking on the words I should be saying.

If only I could force the words past my lips and hand them to him.

He takes a step back, his legs being devoured by inky fingers. "I'm sorry. I'm sure this is creepy. I'll just go now-"

"No!" Bailey suddenly shoots forward and grabs Aryn by the hand, yanking him away from what's hidden beneath the shadows. "Come in, come in. We're just about to watch *Sing*! Hope you love dancing animals and greasy popcorn."

* * *

I somehow end up squished between the two of them, Bailey's eyes trained to the screen with unabashed excitement, while Aryn is quite literally curled into the corner. His entire frame shakes, tremors ricocheting off his skin to mine, and I toss a blanket onto his lap. I can feel his stare and it heats up my entire body, so much so that I must hastily shed my hoodie.

It only takes Bailey approximately 20 minutes into the film to knock out, her hair splayed against the couch's leathery skin and feet tucked under my thighs for warmth. I pause the movie and somehow summon the courage to turn to Aryn.

"Do you want to finish watching this or would you rather watch something else?" I can't tell if my voice waivers.

He continues to stare at the TV screen. "Uhm, this is fine. It's quite upbeat so..." He trails off as if I should know where his mind is right now.

I nod, carefully extracting myself from the plethora of blankets. "I'm going to grab another drink. Want something?"

He pops up, nearly falling over. "I'll come with." His eyes follow my movements before his body does the same. "Is it strange that I'm here? And are you still mad at me?" He leans against the counter, but only in an attempt to hold himself upright. In his current state, he resembles a child recently awakened by a nightmare, rather than a 17-year-old trying to flirt.

I hand him a can of iced tea and shrug. "I'm not going to question our interactions anymore. I'm just going to believe that they happen for a reason, albeit a convoluted one. And no, I'm not mad anymore." He lightly grips my arm before I can head back into the living room.

"Are you saying fate brought us together?"

I examine his face and when I see no indication of sarcasm I step back. "I don't know if I'd describe it like that. But whatever reassures you." As we head back into the living room, I try to calm my breaths and steady my hands. I suppose I also hinted at fate but what does that really mean? Is there already a design laid out for every human; do we not truly get to pick how our lives turn out? Did some cosmic force stuff all of this darkness inside me just for fun?

I play the movie, taking small sips of my tea to keep myself occupied. But Aryn isn't having it. He folds his long legs beneath him and turns to me, eyes latching onto my every breath. I can't help but notice how snug the material fits around his thighs. When he leans in, so close I can smell the subtle aroma of his aftershave, I curl into myself. Why does he unnerve me so much? It's not like he's the first boy to ever try to get close to me. But... he's the only one I've allowed in and I'm going in circles trying to figure out why.

"I honestly didn't mean to offend you the other day. I'm just..." His hands flail like he's trying to conjure the words out of thin air. Then he stops and just covers his face. "Oh god.

112

How can I even explain this to you?"

No doubt a rhetorical question, his silence prompts me to answer him anyway. "You know, nothing like this has ever happened to me before."

Finally, he meets my gaze. "Like what?"

"Perhaps I should rephrase. No one like you has ever entered my life before. There have always been a few guys trying to get into my pants, but none have ever approached me like you have."

He vigorously shakes his head and leans forward again. "No, I am not trying to get into your pants. Please don't think that."

"I know. You're just trying to get under my skin."

"That's not it either!"

This time, I lean into his space and immediately his eyes widen and his ears turn a ridiculous shade of pink. "Then why are you suddenly in my life, in my part of the woods, in the darkness with me?" I press my lips together. "I mean, standing in the dark outside my house?"

If he caught my slip up, he doesn't comment on it. His voice shakes. "I tend to run away from my problems, sometimes literally. Because ignoring them doesn't seem to work."

I take another sip of my tea, the taste now sour. "Don't we all? I don't exactly understand what you're trying to say."

A deep breath and he's diving in again. "That day we met, I was going for a run. I always run in the mornings and always go the same route. But that day I didn't." He scoots forward until his knee touches my thigh. "That's when I met you and since then, even if I don't plan on seeing you, I end up where you are anyway."

There are tiny shocks traveling across my entire body. I propel myself off the couch once again, knocking over the empty cans of tea on the table. I basically sprint to the kitchen, where the stale air cools my burning face.

"I know it's crazy but it's true."

I steady myself against the freezing counter. "I need answers, Aryn. Life is already confusing and messed up as it is; I don't need your semi-romantic bullshit in the equation, too."

He boxes me in, thin but strong arms encasing my entire frame. Just like in the cliché movies. I can simply knock his arm away or duck under it. But I stay and stare at his lips forming the words plucked from somewhere deep inside me.

"Have you ever seen someone, you know, stumbled upon a stranger while shopping or traveling to another city and something just tugs at your chest? It's different from seeing an attractive person because for some reason, when that moment with this stranger passes, it hurts. Like your heart was just stomped on."

His heat is smothering me. In the movies, do these scenes usually end in a kiss?

"I read about this in a book, and it's supposed to signify you meeting your soul mate – it can happen more than once in your lifetime because people can have more than one soulmate and not all are romantic. I haven't ever experienced this feeling until I saw you that day, covered in leaves and dirt." He wears a faint smile but refuses to look at me again.

I shouldn't even be listening to him because things like soulmates, fate and happily ever afters just don't exist. At the end of the day, everything fades and everyone leaves. That's just how the world works. Yet his flushed face and twitching fingers somehow tell me that, although this theory may sound implausible, he needs me to believe it.

"I don't like using terms like soulmates. There is no proof

such things exist. But..." My pause incites his widened eyes to meet mine. "All I know is that that day in the woods did change something. You are always here with me, even when you're not." It's almost a whisper but he grabs my hands and places them against his chest.

"I'm not-" He swallows, starts again. "I'm only asking for your time. Nothing more. I need to know you, need to know if this feeling is real." His heart hammers against his chest.

"But why? Why is this- why am I so important?" He drops his gaze again but I shake my hands loose and lift his chin up. "I need honesty because this," I motion between the two of us. "Is strange. We don't even know one another." I feel like we're going in circles, but nothing is making sense right now. He's too close. He smells like cedar.

"I'm trying so hard to keep myself together and upright." Tears start cascading down his cheeks. I stand there, pulse throbbing. He grips my forearms so tight I wince. But he needs the stability, so I brace myself. "I don't even know if you really exist but please... I need you to be real. I need you to be here. I felt it, I swear to god I felt it that day." He stares into me and I can feel him inside me, scavenging through my dark crevices and clearing cobwebs. "We're both dead inside."

And then we're on the floor, Aryn a bubbling mess of snot and hot tears. He clings to me, fingers digging into my thighs as he collapses against me. He's crumbling; I can feel pieces of him slipping away.

I gather as much of him as I can in my arms. "I'm here and I'm real. You can run to me and I will be here to catch you." I'm making promises I can't possibly keep, but what else am I supposed to do with a dying boy in my lap?

He's already quiet but his body trembles like there is an

earthquake inside him. He leans further into me, like he's trying to bury himself in my empty spaces, and whispers: "Don't hate me. Don't treat me like a monster even though I am one."

"Shh…" I don't understand what he means. I can't grasp this situation or our relationship or what broke the damn inside him. But I'll sort out the jagged pieces in the morning, when my mind is clear and my heart isn't trying to break out of my chest. When it isn't trying to sneak its way into Aryn's palms. So for now, I cradle this broken boy with soft touches and silence. I don't tell him everything will be alright but I remain there, just like he asked. Just how I always imagined someone cradling me.

The darkness stays away that night. Because although Aryn ran to me, he still managed to bring the light with him.

Edge of the World

Aryn

I don't want to get up. Because that requires me dealing with the repercussions of last night, the barrage of questions Savannah is most likely going to ask. The questions I'm not sure I'm ready to answer. I open my eyes anyway, preparing myself for both the onslaught of stale sunlight and Savannah's empty stare.

But I am only greeted by one. The white walls seem to reflect the morning light and I press my palms to my face to shield myself. I quickly open them again, watery eyes visualizing an image my puny brain can't possibly comprehend.

Savannah. Clad in a thin-strapped tank and navy shorts that expose strong thighs. I nearly choke when I realize that she is fast asleep beneath me, as in: I am lying on her chest and curled into her side like a child. I swallow my tongue because she is holding me.

How can anything feel so right? We breathe in sync. I can hear her heartbeat against my ear, irregular but real. I can feel the miniscule prickly hair on her calves and the smooth, dark hair on her forearms. I can see goosebumps erupt along her exposed chest and the corner of her blue bra peeking out from her tank top. She shivers but her body is so warm. I can't stop myself from inching closer; so close that I can feel her blood pulse.

"I didn't expect you to be a cuddler."

I screech like a ravenous pterodactyl and hurl myself off the couch and onto the freezing wood floor. My eyes feel like they might fall out of their sockets, but Savannah just sits up, slowly stretches and smirks at me. I barely see her smile and now she decides to fucking smirk?

"Yeah, well…" I stand up on wobbly legs and half-heartedly motion to her attire. "Why aren't you wearing any clothes?"

She hops off the couch, all skin, cotton and dark eyes. I stare at the ceiling. "I'm allowed to wear whatever I want in my own house." Her arm brushes against mine. Everything tingles. "And out of it, as well."

It's decided: she's sadistic and my pain is her ultimate pleasure.

Still staring at the spotless ceiling, I follow her into the kitchen. There are pieces of me strewn across the tiles. Grey, jagged parts. Savannah narrowly avoids one, a mere tendril really, and pulls out two ceramic mugs. As she starts brewing coffee, I slowly collect my fragments, trying my best to put them back where they belong.

She leans her hip against the counter and stares me down, eyes and mouth still fighting sleep. I brace for impact as her teeth emerge. "I hope you're a coffee person."

All I can do is blink. "What?"

"Coffee. Caffeine. Liquefied energy. I need a cup every morning or I turn into a Romero zombie." She clicks her tongue. "Not a pretty sight, I assure you." The coffee pot gurgles.

I nod, somewhat dumbstruck. "I do. I usually drink two cups in the morning."

The conversation trails off as she fills each mug about ¾ of the way and places them gently, as if they had feelings, on the table. She stares at them, hands hovering above the rising steam, before returning to the cupboards and pulling out a plastic container of blueberry muffins.

I rub the back of my neck. "Uh, where is Bailey?"

Savannah moves swiftly around the kitchen, getting out napkins, utensils and creamer and sugar for the coffee. "She had a date or something with her soon-to-be boyfriend. Sit." She points to the chair I'm already latched onto and takes the one across from me for herself.

Awkward silence pools over us as she takes miniscule sips from her mug and places bits of muffin on her tongue as if catching snowflakes. I stare into my coffee-tinted reflection, inhaling the scent of dark roasted beans, ripe blueberries and uncertainty.

Why are the words suddenly stuck behind my teeth, when last night they fell like melting ice? I can spit words at the reflection in my coffee, but I can't offer words of substance to the enigma in front of me. I can't offer her anything.

I hear her lips part before she even says anything. "I think – hmm…" Eyes averted, she settles the mug against her lips. She doesn't take a sip, but she swallows.

I grip my own mug, starting to feel the aftereffects of shedding built-up tears. "Should I leave?" I don't even realize I'm speaking until she looks up at me, like a frightened and abandoned dog. "I feel like I overstepped some unspoken boundary by spending the night, which wasn't even my initial intention. I just didn't want to be home alone, you know? It's an old house and I swear I hear voices and see strange shapes and–"

Savannah's hand flicks up to silence me.

"Why are you a monster?"

I choke on my tongue, mouth suddenly cottony. After a sip of now lukewarm coffee that chases bubbling dread, I hold my cup like an anchor. "What do you mean?"

"Last night." She refuses to look away and I can't avoid her gaze. "You practically begged me not to hate you. Not to treat you like a monster even though you are one. I don't understand. Why would I hate you?" Now she looks away and trails her finger across the top of her cup, round and round until I'm dizzy just from looking at it.

"I don't know what you're talking about." Denial. Avoidance.

Last night I chose Savannah, instead of Corey or the pain. Last night my bones were straining against my skin and those voices in my head were armed for battle and drunk with rage. Last night... Everything around me was too much yet not enough and I couldn't breathe. I didn't want to. So I came to Savannah in hopes that – what exactly was I hoping for?

While I busy my mouth with pieces of blueberry muffin, I watch Savannah pick apart hers. Her teeth repeatedly dig into her lower lip. "Aryn... you said you came to me because you felt something the day we met. That you need to know I'm real." I can feel her staring at me, but I don't know what her eyes will say if I look back.

My chair scrapes against the floor as I head to the sink. It's quiet again. I almost wince when the cup touches the metal of the sink. I can't bring myself to turn back around and return to the table. But I don't have to; she comes up beside me, so close I can smell her. She makes sure not to touch me.

She whispers against me, "What do you want from me?" When I grip the sink and press my lips together for what feels like hours, she backs away. I suck in a breath. "I need to shower."

I listen to her feet pad across the floor. When I don't hear anything aside from my ragged breathing, I punch my chest and attempt to face the stale insides of Savannah's house. But she's still there, leaning against the doorway with her glistening skin and dark eyes. She clicks her tongue at me.

"Are you ready to go home or...?" She trails off and it takes me a moment to realize that she's not asking me a question: she's telling me I can stay.

I gulp. It echoes around the room and I swear Savannah smirks again. My hands go deep into my jean pockets and curl into fists. "I don't have a toothbrush and I'm sure you don't want to be around my morning breath. Uhm, yeah, perhaps I should just go-"

I don't notice her storming across the room until her hand – smooth and coffee bean scented – is over my mouth and her scent is under my skin. "You sure do talk a lot, you know that?" She slides her hand down until she is cupping my cheek and I lean away, fearing that my now rose-tinted skin will burn hers. She pauses, eyes roaming my face, then leans up, her chest barely grazing mine, and my entire body flushes red. "If I remove my hand," she begins, nose scrunching up. "Will you stop freaking out on me?"

My head moves on its own accord and she immediately falls away from me.

Slowly, she shakes her head and a dislodged curl moves back

and forth with the motion. "I'm not going to force you to talk, because I hate when people do that to me. Just know that when you're ready, I'll actually listen." And she's gone. Out of the kitchen in a blur and all I'm left with is tendrils of her.

* * *

She's in the shower for what seems like an eternity, but when I glance at the clock, I realize it's only been twenty minutes. I should've left, but my feet wouldn't move an inch; I stayed glued to the kitchen counter, counting the tiles and my heartbeats. That's where she finds me and for the first time, I truly catch her off guard. Her eyes, which look even darker now, narrow then widen then narrow again. Her lips turn up before setting into a tiny scowl.

"You are one strange being, Aryn," she breathes, handing me a pile of clothes I just noticed. "These are some of my father's old clothes. I'm sure he won't miss them. You'll have to wear your own boxers, though." She coughs out a warbled giggle and lightly tugs on my sleeve. "I'll show you where my shower is."

"Should I just go home and shower?"

She pauses, back turned to me. Then whispers, "But you may not come back." There is so much pain in her voice that I can't even respond, only follow her.

As she leads me up the stairs, I notice once again that the walls are blank. So white a handprint would surely do ultimate damage. Savannah almost tiptoes up the stairs, blue-socked feet bouncing off the carpet. I focus on that movement, so I don't stare at her clad thighs and exposed back.

"Don't say anything about my room. It's nothing special." She wags her finger at me over her shoulder.

Blue.

I know for certain now that blue is her favorite color. Her bed resembles a tumultuous ocean, deep blue waves rolling across and onto the floor, black splashes of rock or sea creature anchoring the headboard. The furniture itself is dark mahogany, staples of antiquity in revolt against the barrage of sterility infecting the rest of the house. Her curtains are a darker blue, with intricate green and red tulips stitched at random. They are thrown wide open, harsh sunlight reflecting off the sheets as if we truly were in the middle of the sea. Her room is calm, sedated. To a certain extent it's what I expected, but not really what I wanted to see.

Until I turn to the wall opposite her bed. Floor to ceiling there are hundreds of photos tacked up for display. Some are connected to one another by bright string, threads of yellow, red, and orange. Others are overlapping so the images bleed into each other. The photos expand, almost seeming to devour the white walls beneath them. There are photos of graffiti covered vans, of children trying to eat melted ice cream, of a car crash, of a discarded umbrella, of the woods between our houses. There is even one empty spot on the wall, a photo removed from view, the space left behind as clean and lifeless as the white walls downstairs. As if no amount of beauty tacked up can erase the emptiness beneath.

They are all heart wrenching in a way I can't possibly explain, in a way that somehow flips the world on its side. Yet there is one that propels me forward, that makes me clench my jaw. Savannah didn't take this picture; it's sloppy, the lighting is off, but she is the focus of it and that's what makes it the best photo on her wall. She stands at the edge of a cliff, her arms spread out beside her. There is water foaming 50 feet below. Her eyes are closed, hair protruding in all directions. And she is smiling. A barely-there smile that makes my chest throb. Because somehow, I know, just like I knew the day I met her, that if she were alone on that cliff she would jump.

No hesitation. No questions asked or answers given. She would walk off that cliff and disappear into the never-ending blue and wouldn't take a second glance back. Not at those who reached for her. Not at those who screamed her name. Not at me, the person who would probably jump in after her.

Savannah clears her throat. "Is it too much?" She gestures to the wall, her blue socks shuffling against the carpet. "I can see how it'd be a little overwhelming. I just…" She comes to stand next to me, shoulder barely grazing mine, and touches the photo of her. "I *feel* through photos. It's not always easy–" She shakes her head, changes her mind. Backing away from the wall, she grips the edge of her tank. "You want to shower, right?"

Nodding, I follow her into the bathroom. I go through the motions, not really being able to focus on the soothing heat of the water or the smell of Savannah's shampoo. I prolong my shower because I know she's staring at that photo, at that cliff. I know she's wondering why she didn't jump. I know she's thinking of a way to tell me what she couldn't earlier. I know I should ask her why. Why the water is so tempting. Why she looks so happy at the edge of the world. But I know I won't ask. I know I don't want to hear the answer.

Glitter and Tap Water

Savannah

The party is today.

It's been almost an entire week since Aryn slept over and left pieces of himself in my kitchen. But after an awkward exchange of numbers, we've talked almost every day since. We mainly send random texts about the weather or homework assignments. Sometimes we only exchange pictures snapped throughout the day. The one thing that remains a constant is him sending me a good morning text, which, once read, has me immediately sprawled across the cold floor to both cool my burning skin and calm my abnormally thumping heart. Even just imagining his voice messes with my bodily functions.

I look at the message from Abby again, surprised she didn't feel the need to announce the party's arrival in all capital letters like she usually does to express her excitement.

"The party is today." I repeat it to myself, trying to digest what weight the four words truly carry. There have been parties before, the majority of which I've opted out of going to, yet this one is different. Not only because the girls are forcing me to go, but because my own curiosity is propelling me to go, as well.

My phone goes off again, the sound reverberating off all the appliances.

Aryn will be there, too. Dress code is form-fitting dresses or tops that show off some cleavage. Got it?

I quickly snap a picture of what I'm currently wearing and send it to her, too lazy to actually get up and do a full body shot. While waiting for her response, my mind replays that night: Aryn showing up in the middle of the night like a mass murderer sans machete. The crying mess of a boy he became and the monster he claims to be. My promises to be some form of stability, promises I know I can't keep.

I shake my head and struggle to grab the counter's edge, hoisting myself up. Negative thoughts and over-analyzing won't be allowed tonight. I have to keep my mind clear and my hands occupied. If possible, Aryn must be kept at arm's length, not an inch closer.

I'll be over in less than an hour. We're all getting ready at your place. Prepare for a makeover, bitch ;)

What the hell have I gotten myself into?

* * *

Abby didn't just come over. She sauntered in with a flourish of mesh and sequined fabric, stilettos dangling from her fingertips and stuffed in a paper bag, and a smile so devilish she could make every hardened criminal piss their pants.

She discards her war supplies on the floor and points a very red and very sharp index finger at me. "You, young lady, better strap your caramelized ass in." She pushes me onto the couch and presses her mouth right up to my ear. "Are you ready for the most thrilling ride of your life?"

"I don't have health insurance so please don't injure me with all those trinkets and toys."

Her laugh sends shivers down my spine. "Oh, honey. I'm not going to hurt you. I'm just going to prod you until you become completely submissive to my every wish and desire." She claps her hands together and starts laying out the clothing she brought.

"I'm not entirely sure what's going on but-"

"No buts! I am merely here to make sure Aryn not only notices you but makes a move. Tonight is when Savannah, newly reformed sex goddess, makes her debut." She holds up a black strapless dress that looks like it was made for a child and grins like the Cheshire. "Isn't this exciting?"

I nod, voicelessly watching as she delicately lines the heels she brought up against the wall opposite me. They ascend from shortest heel to tallest, matte to sparkly.

I clear my throat to catch her attention. "Not that I don't enjoy this, uh... quality time with you, but when are Bailey and Jacklyn getting here?"

"Soon enough, darling. Jacklyn had to get gas and I think they're also picking up some wine coolers and pizza. We're going to pre-game here." She turns to wink at me. "Not that we're trying to get drunk or anything."

Unconvinced but fully aware that arguing is futile, I bob my head up and down.

I stare at the army of heels against the wall, wondering which one is pointy enough to use as a weapon. Or perhaps I should impale myself on one. There is even a pair with metal spikes along the toe portion. That in itself is a hazard, so someone must have predicted their design would one day be used for a homicide.

"I brought a lot of options for you." She clasps her hands together, as if in prayer. "But these... these are the top contenders." Motioning to three outfits displayed on the couch opposite me, she giggles then pulls me up.

The first is a red halter top paired with a black, layered skirt. She put a pair of red, strappy sandals on the floor beneath them. The second is a very tight-looking strapless black dress, plain overall expect for the skin-like material. What looks to be suede booties rest beneath. The third option calls my name and I have to pick it up. The blue material is soft to the touch and reminds me of frothy waves in early morning light. Even the lace stitched into the midriff area feels silky beneath my fingers.

"I knew it. I knew you were going to pick this dress." She picks up the small, white pumps off the floor and tucks them under her arm. "I never wore it so please, take it if you want it."

I bring the dress to my chest, savoring the feel of something so smooth against my skin.

"Thank you, Abby. It's perfect."

* * *

Time to myself means time to nitpick. To resize, reexamine, question. When Abby decides to quickly run to the nearest Starbucks – "I literally need sugar or I'll die" is what she said – my body instinctively gravitates to the cool blue of my room.

I stare at myself in the mirror, hair sticking up in random places, a mane of dark curls that softly frame my face, stick to my sweaty skin and caress my cheeks like someone's hands should. My clothes, though not yet wrinkled nor emanating sweat fueled bio, suddenly feel dirty. My knees start to ache and the muscles contract across my stomach.

I step back, step out of my shorts, slip off my shirt, out of my skin. Bare. Cells and nerves and tissue. Is that all we really are? The parts of us, they disconnect, bend and break, but do they ever truly fit together? Are we ever truly whole?

This body, which others call mine and sometimes claim to be theirs, feels heavy naked, perhaps heavier than when clothed. My bones seem to expand outwards, straining desperately against my skin. Skin that is marred by what others see, believe, and deny. Skin that has taken the blame for what my mind deems wrong, blame I cannot stop choosing to claim.

For a second, the mirror appears to quiver and rattle atop the metal foundation. But when I breathe that is what's reflected, uneven breaths rocking my frame and not the mirror's. I cross my arms across my chest, eyes tightly closed as I grip my shoulders and try to pull the splinters of myself back inside. I calm, settle into the body. Salt invades my mouth. Once open, my eyes stare at a mess of a being. Puffy face, lackluster complexion, ever expanding hair. My hips don scarlet smiles, lipstick marks from random shiny things – scissors, knives, safety pins. Seeing them allows me to relax my shoulders, breathe in and breathe out. Seeing them causes me to gag and grip myself tighter.

Sliding my palms down my body, I shiver. Even these hands feel foreign. I take one more glance at me, her, this concoction of flesh and bones, then slip on the dress.

It puts pressure in all the right places, keeps me contained. Air just gushes out of me and I'm able to turn away from the mirror. Just as I do, the front door slams open and I know that my time alone, as much as it hurts, is over.

"Oooh, that dress looks nice on you. Not as tight as I hoped but beggars can't be choosers, now can they?" Abby wraps her arms around my waist and squeezes. "I am going to explode from all the excitement."

I wiggle out of her grasp and throw myself back onto the couch. "Don't get your insides all over the place. Glitter is actually quite hard to clean up."

She clicks her tongue at me. "Well, aren't you funny." Her fingers demolish her phone's screen as she sends out a text or updates a status. "Jacklyn and Bailey just picked up the pizza and will be here in like 10 minutes." She squints at her screen. "The party starts at 9 so we have roughly three hours before it's socially acceptable to show up."

"So we're just going to eat and drink for the next three hours?"

"Oh, Savannah." Her palms repeatedly slide against my hair, mimicking a petting motion. "Hair and makeup are going to take at least an hour. I'm going to shower here because I need to shave again." Abby shivers. "God forbid I have any stubble tonight."

I lean back and watch as she fumbles once more through her bag of goodies. To my surprise, she picks out a pair of ripped jeans and a dark red halter top. Singling out a matching set of stilettos, she winks (now that I think about it, is it a twitch?) and heads for the stairs. I hear the shower turn on not even 30 seconds later and I unclench my muscles.

Staring at the clothes strewn across my living room, the light bouncing off every stitched sequin, I start to feel the last few pieces of muffin crawling up my throat. I suddenly find myself standing over the kitchen sink, gulping in air. The harder I grip the counter, the less anxious I feel, even though my fingers start to ache. I think I stand like that for ten minutes before sliding to the floor, a spot my body seems to crave lately.

A yelp – or perhaps a guttural groan – is ripped from my stomach when my phone rings. His name pops up, faceless on the screen but oh so vibrant in my mind.

"Hello?"

"Hey you."

The muffin, now settled in the pit of my stomach, suddenly feels hard as a rock.

"I need to find an appropriate ringtone for you. I almost had a heart attack when my phone rang."

Aryn's laugh turns into a cough. "Well, so yeah, I hope it's okay that I'm calling you. I just wanted to uh, check if you're coming to the party tonight. I didn't see you at school this entire week so I couldn't ask."

I try to suppress a sigh. "I'll be there. Against my will, of course, but it should be fun. Maybe."

"That's great!" He sighs, too but it sounds way different than mine. "Do you know what time you'll arrive? I'll make sure to save you the good alcohol." He laughs, but it sounds forced.

"I don't drink but thanks." Well, I can't drink, but he doesn't need to know that.

Brief pause. "That's good to know. Don't take anything from anyone then, okay? They spike everything!"

"Even water?"

I receive a real laugh this time and can't help but smile. His laugh reminds me of the tide. "There is tap water, of course.

But don't leave your cup anywhere. Oh!" He fumbles with the phone and whispers "shit" before clearing his throat. "Do you want me to bring you an iced coffee? When I'm not in the mood to drink, I usually bring a coffee or iced tea to sip on. That way no one asks me if I want a beer or shot or anything."

I take a deep breath and bring my knees to my chest, a tactic I find extremely useful when talking to Aryn. "That would be amazing. Thank you so much. I'll pay you back."

"Don't worry about it. So I'll see you around…" He trails off and I realize I never answered his question.

"We'll be there around 9:30, I think."

"Gotcha. Can't be anything but fashionably late, right?" I hum in response because I don't know what constitutes as being fashionably late. "Okay, I'll let you go. See you in few hours!"

He hangs up both before I can say anything in return and before the front door swings open with the clinking of wine coolers.

I don't even have time to say hello before Abby comes rushing down the stairs screeching, her towel barely covering her goods.

"Who's ready to party, bitches?!"

I don't know if I am, but this is the first time I've wanted to be.

Run to You

Aryn

"Are you ready yet?"

My head moves on its own accord, first nodding then redirecting itself from left to right. "There is no true preparation for an encounter with Savannah." I run my hands through my hair then down my face. "Does my hair look okay? Should I brush it again or add gel?" I push both items in front of Corey's face, but he groans and smacks them to the floor.

"Will you stop worrying about every single detail? I highly doubt Savannah will care how you look, especially because she's probably imagining burying you somewhere in the woods."

"For the last time, she's not a serial killer."

He sucks his teeth, dismissing my comment with a flip of his hand. "Besides, it's a pool party so your hair is going to get wet anyway! So let's go, yeah?"

I fasten the top two buttons on my shirt, look in the mirror, immediately regret it and unbutton them again. "Yeah, I guess I'm ready. But don't forget that we have to go to Dunkin' before the party."

Corey tilts his head and then chuckles. "Right, to get her coffee. I guess we should both get something then, too."

"Why?"

"Oh, Aryn," he places his hands on my shoulders. "You really don't know anything about dating. If you only show up with a drink for her, she's going to think you're trying too hard."

I shrug his hands off. "But I am and she already knows that."

"Pssh, fine. Then maybe don't let everyone else know it, too. We've made it this far into our high school careers without being the victims of dating gossip and childish rumors."

"Yeah, yeah. I'm craving an Americano anyway."

He pushes me through my front door and slams it behind him. "I wonder what kind of donuts they'll have available now. I could really go for a glazed."

* * *

Twenty minutes later and my car smells like freshly brewed coffee and fried dough. When we pull up to John's house – well, more accurately an oversized, all glass structure – the music from inside drowns out my car's stereo.

I hear Corey's jaw drop. "What, did he invite the entire school? Damn!" He struggles to unbuckle himself and open the door at the same time, despite the fact that the car is still moving. "All the good alcohol is going to be gone if we don't hurry!" I finally pull onto an empty patch of lawn and he bolts, screaming, "I'll save you a shot!"

In no rush to be bombarded by 200 plus drunk high schoolers, I take a few deep breaths to calm my nerves, rub my already sweaty palms on my jeans, and collect the precious, coffee-infused cargo. I make sure to stuff Savannah's surprise, wrapped carefully in the thin, brown Dunkin' napkins, into my jacket pocket. Then I start weaving my way through those roaming outside, clinking beer bottles like they are at a dinner party and having what appears to be dance battles.

When I get inside, I can barely hear myself think. Whoever created the playlist chose songs with the deepest bass. There is hardly a gap of silence between songs; they quickly play in succession as if they are chasing one another.

Neither Corey or I are very tall so locating him among the masses takes a few minutes of going up on my tiptoes and arching my neck. When I see him, I grab him by his shirt collar.

"Dude, you can't just disappear like that."

He whips around, two red solo cups in his hands. Lifting one to his mouth, he grins. "I got us vodka, bro! The last of it!"

Silently, I take one cup from him, pour it into the other, and stack my now empty cup under his. "Designated driver. No drinking and driving, didn't they teach you that in school?" He answers by chugging the cup, burping immediately after. "You're disgusting!" I wrap him in a headlock and proceed to drag him toward the patio, where the pool is.

"No one is swimming," Corey says, forcing my arm from around his neck to his shoulders. "It's too cold, I guess..."

There are plenty of people out here, but they all stand a safe distance away from the water. A few sit on the chairs lining the pool, but other than that, it's like the water is off limits. "Maybe I should have gotten her a large. Or a latte. I don't know." I shake the cup a little and sigh when I hear the ice cubes clink against one another. Looking around, I grip Corey tighter. "She should be here soon."

"Dude, are you really that nervous?"

"Should I not be?"

He turns to face me and purses his lips. "I really thought this was just some like, weird knight in shining armor thing. But I was wrong, huh?"

"At first, I was definitely intrigued because she seemed so lost. I mean, she is still extremely distant and in her own world, but it's more than that. I can't really explain what it is yet, but she... I like what I've seen of her so far."

"Or what she decided to show you."

I shake the coffee again, liking both the sound and the condensation running down my fingers. "I just need to show her she can trust me. I hope she can trust me."

The music suddenly prevents any possibility of talking and Corey and I just sway to the beat, not really dancing but moving with the crowd. When the breeze picks up, smelling of freshly cut grass and something sweet, something I can just taste on the tip of my tongue, I close my eyes and release the built-up tension. I can hear every sound around me, beer sloshing in their bottles, the low laughter of a couple in the trees, the clicking of heels. The music vibrates through me and it almost tickles. This moment, this cacophony of sounds and smells, almost reminds me of a lullaby.

I'm jerked back to reality when my arm is tugged, the deafening bass washing away any moment of peace. Corey, mouth moving a mile a minute, is pointing behind me. I squint my eyes in an effort to focus on his mouth and the words it's forming.

"She's here!"

Those are the only two words I need to hear. Turning around

seems to take an hour, like my body can't catch up to my mind. I've already imagined an entire conversation with her when my legs and torso finally end up facing the right direction.

"Oh shit." It comes out involuntarily, but it's the only thing my mouth can say as I look at her. I say it about a million times before Corey, quite literally, slaps me across the face.

"Instead of saying 'shit,' why don't you actually go talk to her and give her the damn coffee that you've been holding onto like some sort of trophy?"

My feet don't fail me, but now it's my brain that can't seem to catch up. Too much stimuli, too many 'what if' scenarios flitting through my head. I somehow remember the balled-up napkins in my pocket and manage to pull it out without squishing it any further. I reach her and before anyone can say anything, I hand her the coffee and napkin bundle.

"You look beautiful." My voice sounds weak, but I can tell my words make an impact as Savannah pulls her arms into her chest.

"Thank you. For the coffee and..." She carefully removes each layer of napkin. "Ah, a blueberry muffin! How did you know I like these?"

Stuffing my hands into my pockets and focusing on her face, I shrug. "We had them for breakfast at your place last weekend."

Her mouth wears a different shape today. Almost a smile, almost a grimace. It is hard not to look at every part of her. From her ever-expanding curls to her slightly crooked feet and slim ankles. The blue dress she wears bears a striking resemblance to the tulip she slept with in the forest and the picture of the waves on her wall. I feel my knees begin to shake.

137

"Hi, Aryn." Bailey, Jacklyn and Abby are all staring at me. There is a little less malice in their eyes this time, but they're not exactly overjoyed to see me. At least Bailey offers me a smile and says, "You look nice tonight."

My eyes immediately snap to Savannah as I tug on my sleeves, awaiting her response. I watch as she looks me up and down, looking away when she meets my gaze.

"You do. But workout clothes don't look so bad, either." She bites the straw, but I can see the corners of her mouth turning up. I allow myself to straighten and direct a smile at the girls.

"Thank you. Jacklyn, Corey is around here somewhere." I turn to scan the crowd and find him barely ten feet away, eyes wide like a child in a candy store. "But beware," I say, shaking my head. "He already had a full cup of straight vodka."

She begins to run in his direction, arms spread wide like a mother welcoming her child home. Meanwhile Abby, tugging on her top, says something about finding her next conquest. I raise my eyebrows, but both Bailey and Savannah shrug and watch as Abby saunters – quite literally – back into the house.

"I'm going to go find Jack." She wraps one arm around Savannah's waist. "Just text me if you need me, okay?"

Then it's just the two of us, three feet apart, surrounded by thirty drunk teenagers. I clear my throat, but no words come out so I merely gesture to the nearby lawn chairs. We sit down, the only important sound coming from her sipping on her coffee. Her muffin is almost all gone.

"I didn't realize our entire class and some underclassmen would be here." Her voice is low but solid and I can't help but notice how her entire body angles inward.

"Uhm, yeah. John is quite notorious for throwing over-the-top parties. Endless booze, loud music, and way too many people."

She stares over my shoulder to where people are coming in and out of the house. "I was actually looking forward to coming tonight but if I'm being honest…" She bites her lip, shoves the rest of the muffin in her mouth and takes a long sip of her coffee. Even when she's done chewing, she remains silent.

I face her completely, trying my best to block the people from her view. "Savannah, you can always be honest with me."

She looks at me, not past me or through me, but into me. She doesn't look away. "It's a little overwhelming. I just… I'm nervous, I guess."

Nodding, I inch even closer. There are less voices behind us, but the music continues to penetrate our conversation. "I can take you home if you'd like? I haven't had any alcohol."

She slowly shakes her head. "I've only just arrived."

"You aren't obligated to stay. It's just a dumb high school party. They aren't that important."

Again, she looks at me. A lopsided smile faces me. "You don't know my friends." She scoffs and places her cup on the ground. Tucking her legs beneath her, she turns to face me. I have to lean back an inch so she won't notice how red my ears are turning. "Abby insisted that I come tonight and finally become a sex goddess or whatever."

I choke on my tongue. "A what?"

Her eyes widen and she turns so her curls cover part of her face. "Forget I said anything."

"No, no. I'm sorry. I just… Why does she want you to become a sex goddess? Or whatever?"

Her shoulders rise and get eaten by her hair. "She's a weirdo." She abruptly turns to me, eyes narrowed. "Do you know how many hours she made us walk around the mall just so she could find the 'perfect bathing suit'?" She uses air quotes for emphasis. "Four hours, Aryn. Four long and humiliating hours." When she throws her head back, her neck elongates and her collarbones – of all things – make the red spread from my ears to my neck. What the fuck is wrong with me?

To bury myself deeper in hormonal hell, I point to the pool. "I hope you didn't spend a lot on a bathing suit. No one is actually swimming." I await her answer, secretly hoping she says she did and that she's going to swim anyway and that I should swim with her. But she glances at the pool and makes a humming noise deep within her throat. I chuckle, "What? Did you forget to bring your bathing suit to a pool party?"

"No, not exactly."

I lightly kick her chair. "What? You can tell me."

Tucking some flyaway curls behind her ear, she purses her lips. "Well, you see-" There is a splash and we both turn to look at the few courageous drunkards cannonballing into the pool.

"Well I guess it's officially a pool party now!" I grin at her and stand up. "Shall we go? No need to be embarrassed anymore-"

"I can't swim!" She blurts it out, pulling me back down onto my chair. She grips my hand so tightly it actually starts to hurt. After a few beats of not-so-silence, she loosens her grip, but doesn't let go completely. "It *is* embarrassing and if you're going to make fun of me, just go ahead and do it."

I just stare at her bent head, running sentences through my brain and trying to find the right one. Finally, I settle on one: "Not knowing how to swim isn't that embarrassing. And to make fun of you would be a shit move on my part."

Still not looking up, she whispers, "Do you mean that?"

I place my hand over hers, reeling from the fact that she's actually allowing me to touch her. That she is touching me. "Of course. But I'd love to know why you never learned, if you're willing to tell me."

She raises her head and I can tell she's trying to avoid looking at the pool. She clears her throat. "When I was little, I drowned. Apparently, I was dead for like a whole two minutes. Aside from my parents becoming paranoid about me being near water, I was always too scared to try learning and now I freak out when I get too close." She laughs a little. "Which is ironic because apparently I used to love being in the water and I love the ocean. Well, I love looking at it."

I let her take a few deep breaths before tightening my hold on her hand. I make sure she's looking at me. "You don't ever need to be embarrassed about what scares you. A trauma like that can last a lifetime and anyone who makes you feel less because of it, well they're assholes and don't deserve the time of day anyway."

I try my best to focus on this moment, our hands intertwined and her eyes on me and only me. But I can't help thinking about the picture of her on that cliff, arms spread, water lapping below. Was she scared then even though she looked so content? Why does her not fearing death make so much sense?

She just nods and presses her fingers against my palm. I stand, gently letting go of her hand. "How about I get you a drink. Tap okay?"

"Perfect." I see her smile, slight yet so vibrant and I have to power walk away.

The lights inside momentarily blind me and I bump into a few people before finally finding my way into the kitchen. While filling up two cups with water, the music changes from something fast-paced to a middle school slow dance song. I almost want to ask Savannah to dance, but I like the atmosphere we created for ourselves outside. Besides, the makeshift dance floor – John's living room – is to full capacity and no one is slowing down anyway.

Securing a cup in each hand, I turn to go back outside but come face to face with a visibly pulsating Corey.

"Corey, dammit! Can you not always sneak up on people? I'm going to end up dying of a heart attack before I reach 20."

He reaches behind me and produces a full bottle of red wine. Cork already unscrewed, he brings the bottle to his lips and inhales about a quarter of it in 15 seconds. "Man, I have so much energy right now! I feel like I could... I could lift a fucking truck!" To emphasize this statement, he flexes his miniscule arm muscles.

I attempt to wrestle the wine bottle from him. "You need to slow down. Maybe have some water and food. Here." I hand him one of the cups of water. "Just drink this. All of it."

Surprisingly, he complies, although he does manage to spill quite a bit of it on himself. Only slightly satisfied, I locate the nearest solid food and hand him a bowl of pretzels. Without question, he shoves a handful into his mouth and stares at me as he chews.

"You know," he starts, still chewing. "You're such a good friend. I really hope things are going well with Savannah." He takes another swig of the wine and burps. "Where is she by the way?"

"Yeah, where is she?"

I jump, the voice coming from right over my shoulder. Bailey stands beside me, holding hands with a guy I can only assume to her boyfriend, Jack. He smiles, emitting a vibe much friendlier than that of Bailey's other companions.

Jacklyn sidles up to Corey and somehow manages to hide the wine from his view. "Savannah tends to wander off by herself quite a lot. You gotta keep an eye on that one." Again, they refer to Savannah like she's a child. A child who hasn't learned to stay away from fire or know when to call out stranger danger.

"Yeah... I was just getting us some water. Oh, speaking of which," I fill up another cup, taking a sip to quench my dry throat. "I should get back to her. She's still outside on the patio."

Jack, suddenly becoming animated, groans. "Man, you better be careful out there. Rumor has it that one tradition for John's infamous pool parties is that if you're by the pool, you're getting pushed or thrown in. No exceptions."

I grimace, taking another sip from my cup. "That's idiotic. Can these people even swim if they're so drunk?"

Bailey laughs, "That's why the majority of people stay inside! I guess a fight broke out last year because someone pushed someone else in and their phone got absolutely destroyed." She shrugs, leaning closer to Jack. "Teenage antics. What can you do?"

We are all silent for a moment, sipping at our drinks and watching the drunk people try to dance without falling. Something tugs at the back of my mind, like I should be doing or remembering something. There is a scream from outside, loud enough to be heard over the ever-increasing music.

Jack laughs, slapping the nearby kitchen counter. "See, I told you! No one is safe."

But that scream didn't sound like a spirited stop-playing-around plea. It sounded like the ground was just ripped from beneath someone's feet.

Bailey straightens up. "Wait a minute," she starts walking toward the pool, slowly, as if she just realized something. "You said Savannah was out there?"

It takes me two seconds of recognition, two seconds that seem to last two hours, before I sprint toward the patio. I push everyone out of my way, accidently knocking one guy to the floor. There is no time to apologize because I don't hear anymore screams or laughter, just splashing water.

Before I jump, I look over to the lawn chairs. To where we held hands only minutes before. But I don't see a mane of hair or an ocean-blue dress. I don't see her or feel her. So I jump without even looking.

I frantically look around, the chlorine burning my eyes and bubbles breaking my vision. Fortunately, it is only her and me in the water at the moment, though so I locate her easily, flailing and grasping at the water. Pushing through the water, I reach her and brace myself for her struggle and panic. She pulls away, opens her mouth to scream, and then propels her body into mine. She tightens her grip on my shoulders and wraps her legs around my waist. She stills. I can feel her heart against my chest.

I break the surface, securing Savannah's head above the water before swimming to the edge. She's gasping for air, but she's still breathing. She's crying. Corey and Jack help pull her out of the water and I'm momentarily halted by the crowd. They all just stare. A few have their phones out.

"She could've died! And you all just stood there!"

Murmurs, faces contorting, people walking away.

"Hey, man," A guy slowly walks up to me, hands out in front of him in defense. He's bare chested and soaking wet. "I'm so sorry. I didn't know she couldn't swim. I swear I wouldn't have thrown her in otherwise."

I walk up to him, fists shaking and knees trembling. "But you still stood there and watched her struggle to stay afloat, right?" I hear Savannah coughing behind me, and I take a step back. "Just get out of here before I decide to drown you myself." He scampers away and the other bystanders avoid my gaze while retreating inside.

I return to Savannah's side, but she's already surrounded by Jacklyn, Bailey and Jack. Corey stands a little to the side, glaring at anyone who tries coming out to the patio. I bend down, trying to meander my way to Savannah.

"Savannah, I am so sorry. I came as fast as I could."

Jack moves away, instead taking a place behind Bailey. Savannah looks like a beautiful drowned lion, still emitting waves of defiance even though she's shivering and curled into a tiny ball. Someone managed to wrap her in a large towel, which she clings to.

She swats away Bailey's and Jacklyn's hands, rubbing her wrinkled fingers against her trembling lips. "This is what happens when no one listens to me." She begins to dig her nails into her arms, and I'm reminded of bloodied mud. "You can all stay but I want to go home. Now."

Bailey helps her stand up and begins to lead her around the side of the house, but Savannah pulls away. "Sav, come on. I'll take you back to my place."

But she shakes her head, wet locks sticking to her cheeks. "I want to go back to my house." And then she looks at me, dark eyes anything but terrified. "Please."

* * *

The entire way back, she is completely silent. She only spoke once before getting into my car and it was to ask, "Aren't I going to get your seats all wet?" After telling her it didn't matter, she curled up on the passenger seat, leaned her head against the window, and didn't utter one word to me. I drove a little over the speed limit because I didn't want her to get sick. At least she stopped shivering once I blasted the heat.

Before we turn down the long dirt path that branches into two smaller roads, one leading to her house and the other leading to mine, she stretches out and turns to me. It's too dark in the car to see her eyes.

"I lied."

I slow down and wait for her to continue. When we reach the fork in the road, I stop the car. "What did you lie about?"

She heaves a sigh, as if talking takes all the energy out of her. "I don't want to go to my house."

Turning on the lights inside the car, I quickly put the car in park. "Well where do you want to go then?"

She turns back to the window and stares into the darkness.

"Savannah, please. You are soaking wet. You need to get changed into something dry." I begin to turn down her driveway, the rocks bouncing off my tires.

Suddenly she grabs my forearm, fingers viciously shaking. Her voice is in slivers. "Please don't take me to that house." It seems that is all she can say because she only proceeds to point to the path on our left.

I look at the soggy towel and her dripping dress before I meet her eyes. I try to focus on her face, instead of her fear. Her face; no creasing lines, no sly smiles, none of the usual voids or trickery.

"Why?"

I hope to see something cross her face when she answers, but she merely loosens her grip on my arm. The towel pools in her lap. Her jaw is tense and her fingernails dig once again into her arms and I reverse without question, my car lurching down the darkened path. Savannah slides down the seat as we drive further away from her house.

We enter my house on tiptoes, because it's almost 11 and both my mom and sister are asleep by now. I briefly pause in front of my room. Even Corey hardly ever comes in here; am I really going to let Savannah in? What am I actually trying to hide? My dirty boxers? Savannah tugs on the back of my shirt and whispers against my shoulder.

"I don't care if it's messy. I just want to change because I'm freezing."

Holding my breath, I push open the door and quickly turn on the light. She scurries in after me, carefully closing the door behind us. Shivering, she examines my room, eyes lingering momentarily on the plaid boxers strewn across my desk chair. Was I expecting a skeleton to pop out from under my bed and list out the things I've done wrong in life?

"Sorry, sorry." I crumble them into a ball and stuff them into my clothes hamper. Then I rummage through my dresser, pulling out a blue t-shirt, a brand-new pair of boxers and an old pair of sweatpants. "I actually never wear these, so if they're comfortable you can keep them." She holds everything in front of her and follows me across the hallway into the bathroom. "I've never worn the boxers either."

She snorts, color already coming back into her cheeks. "That's good to know." The clothes are hanging limp at her side now. "It's like we're taking turns. You sleep over at my house and shower and now I'm showering at yours and sleeping with you. Weird."

I don't think she meant to word it that way, but it still makes my hands tremble. "Okay, so you can use anything you want. There's shampoo and conditioner here. The body wash, unfortunately, is uh, marketed for men. My sister and mom use another bathroom."

She places the clothes on the toilet and then slumps against the sink. She looks ragged, drawn out, but not as shaky as she did in the car. "I don't mind smelling like you for a night."

I drop the body wash and fumble to set it back upright. Placing a towel on the sink next to her, I remind her that my room is right across the hall and bolt out the door. But my legs can only carry me so far and I find myself standing beside the bathroom door. I hear Savannah shuffling around, little sniffles filling the room before she turns on the shower. My chest pounds and I have to fan my face. Closing my eyes, I listen to the water run before dragging myself away.

When she comes in, I try not to stare. The sweatpants look like they belong to her, not too tight but definitely more form-fitting than they would have been on me. She has her arms across her chest, almost clutching the shirt, but it still billows away from her torso. I can smell the shampoo and body wash wafting off her. I don't remember ever smelling that good.

"I just laid my wet stuff over the shower rod. I hope that's okay."

"Definitely. Does everything fit okay?"

She nods, sitting at the edge of the bed. "Can I also have a pair of socks?" She scratches her cheek. "My feet get so cold." After tossing her a pair, she stretches out her legs on the bed and wiggles her toes. She throws a grin in my direction, although it stretches her mouth into an odd shape. "I think I pull you off pretty well."

I laugh, trying to make her feel at ease, then I get up to grab an extra blanket and turn off the lights. "Now, now. Let's not be hasty. I still have to teach you my ways."

She climbs beneath the covers, nothing but her eyes and wet hair visible. "It's okay that we're sharing the bed, right?"

"Of course." I flip the light switch and then fumble back to the bed. I accidently kick her when I slid beneath the covers. "Sorry, and also, I don't know if I snore or not so just be prepared."

She shifts her weight and I can feel her breath on my face. "You do and it's unbearable. But no worries, I move a lot so you may wake up with a few bruises."

"Yeah, I'm pretty sure you fractured a rib when I was at your house."

We lie there in the dark, covered in silence. The moon is so bright tonight that if I were to look over at her, I would be able to see everything that happened today etched onto her face. My hand twitches with the urge to grab her hand again and press my fingers into her palm like she did earlier.

"Thank you, Aryn." Her voice is so soft I feel like I almost imagine it.

"What for?"

I feel her jump. "Oh god, I thought you were sleeping." I sense her hand reaching out for me before I can actually feel it.

I hold it against my chest, trying to decide between weaving my fingers through hers or leaving everything as is. "You don't have to thank me."

She halts, suddenly becoming stock-still. "Of course I do. You saved me."

I try catching her eye, but she has receded beneath the comforter. "You're welcome, although I really wish it didn't happen." She makes a sound in the back of her throat but doesn't say anything in return. "And I already told you."

Her head pops up from beneath the burrow of pillows and blankets. "What did you tell me?"

"That I'd always run to you." She tries to burrow her face back into the pillow, but I gently grab her chin. "Don't hide from me. Not after today, not after we're already in bed together." It's a joke, but she scowls at me.

"Oh, stop it. This is serious."

I take her hand off my chest and place it against my cheek, so she can feel my words. "I know it is. I... I thought I was going to lose you. You just came into my life and we're still figuring out everything between us and it's... I ran as fast as I could."

She moves toward me, until her chest is almost touching mine. "I thought I was going to die. I was terrified and I didn't know which way was up or down. But then I *felt* you and..." She gulps, her face overtaken by an expression I haven't seen yet. "Suddenly, I knew I was safe. I knew you wouldn't let me go."

I slide my hand against her hair until I reach the back of her neck. Gauging her reaction, I slowly lean forward and press my forehead against hers. "Never."

Her lips are trembling and my instinct is not to kiss her, although I've never wanted to kiss someone as badly as I do her. Instead, I remove my hand from her neck and gently run my thumb across her lips. She sucks in air, but her lips stop trembling. I lean back, letting go of every part of her I'm touching. But she follows me and lays her head against my chest.

"I could see myself running to you, too." She wraps one tense arm around my waist and sighs. "None of this makes sense. I keep trying to figure out why I'm so comfortable around you. Why touching you feels like-" She groans, lightly slamming her forehead into my chest.

I finger curls that somehow escaped her bun. "What does touching me feel like?" I hold my breath, not wanting to miss a single word. She leans on her elbow, still facing me but too far away. She is illuminated by the moonlight and I can't take my eyes off her.

"I want to puke when people touch me. I don't know why, it just feels wrong, like my body and mind are arguing over what I need. But getting close to you, feeling you next to me..." Her eyes suddenly close. "Comforting you comes easily to me."

I can't resist the urge to take her hands in mine again. I complete what she didn't say. "Even this, holding your hand, it feels so right. I'm not afraid or anxious. No one has ever made me feel this way before so whatever we have between us..." I pause, not really knowing how to finish the sentence. Instead, I run my hand down her arm and smooth out the goosebumps.

She just nods, neither of us being able to put it into words. I slide back beneath the covers and she follows suit. I'm wide awake, but her soft breathing begins to lull me to sleep. Savannah tightens her grip on my waist. I'm drifting, eyelids heavy and muscles relaxed. Maybe I'm dreaming, but I swear I hear her speak.

"I know you," she suddenly whispers. "I *knew* you. You're the boy in the picture."

Monster

Savannah

Everything hurts. The tips of my fingers and toes tingle, that fuzzy half-asleep feeling that simultaneously tickles and aches. I attempt to lift my arms, but it feels like there is a rubber band attaching them to my torso and hips. Staring out the window, I challenge the sun until my eyes water. Then I manage to turn onto my back, an involuntary groan crawling up my throat, and reach out to the other side of the bed. I don't realize what I'm reaching for until I don't feel anything.

I stare at the cool, empty space beside me. So very empty. Has my own bed ever felt this large before? So incapable of being filled by one body? I crawl to his side, gripping the sheets tightly with my numb fingers until I'm finally occupying space that is not mine. I bury my face into the pillow, aching for any indication that he was here, that I was not alone. There is a hint of his shampoo, or maybe it is merely my imagination, but I breathe it in anyway and curl up beneath the covers.

He kept me close during the night, my skin sticking to his under the warmth of the sheets. I melted into him, never feeling so at ease during the night. But his grip got progressively tighter throughout the night; his breathing ragged and laced with whimpers. So as much as I yearned for his arms around me, I turned onto my back and pulled him into me. I cradled him, like I did that day in my kitchen, until he was silent.

Although well-rested, I can still feel myself drifting, being pulled back under. That's when I hear footsteps. Even, heavy with purpose. They pause, right before entering the room, and the person clears their throat.

We just stare at one another for what feels like an eternity before he shuffles in, a tray in his hands, and softly pushes the door closed with his foot. He sits at the edge of the bed, an inch too far from where I am cocooned. I still can't feel him.

"I brought you breakfast. Wasn't sure you wanted to meet my mom and baby sister yet, so…" He trails off, clearing his throat again.

I try to sit up, but my body fails me and a spasm slides down my spine. I don't realize I've made any noise until Aryn kneels in front of me.

"What's wrong? Are you hurt?" His fingers hover over my body, trying to find the pain without actually touching me.

I lean toward him, head falling forward until it reaches his neck. "I'm sore. Can you help me sit up?"

I lean into him as he places his hands on my sides. The pressure from his grip hurts, but it's a good kind of pain. The type of pain that lets me know this is real.

Once propped up, he places the tray of food on my lap, a large grin extending from ear to ear. "I made the pancakes myself. We even had blueberries so I put some into the mix."

I stare at the plate, filled with pancakes, fruit, and sausage.

There is even a glass of orange juice and a mug of coffee. I lift the mug first, coffee always a priority for breakfast, and stare into the liquid. Then I take a sip and feel at home. "You... How did you know how I like my coffee?"

His ears are red. "Uhm, I remember from that day at your house. You put two spoons of sugar and you measured a tablespoon of creamer..." He looks away from me.

I look down at the mug. "You noticed all of that?"

The red is spreading to his neck now. My own cheeks begin to heat up, although I can't pinpoint a reason as to why. "Of course I did. I pay attention to you, Sav."

I bit the inside of my cheek, not used to having someone look at me like he's looking at me now. "Thank you."

He sits down, this time cross-legged on the side of the bed I slept on. He's not looking at me, so I take the time to follow the reddening of his skin as it travels below his shirt. It's my favorite shade of red and I would paint all the rooms that color if I could.

My stomach gurgles, perhaps with hunger, perhaps with a jumbled mess of hormones.

I stuff a piece of pancake in my mouth and a blueberry bursts. Within minutes, the entire plate looks as if it was just washed and my stomach, which hasn't been filled like this in months, almost purrs. I lick my lips once more, remove the tray from my lap, and turn to Aryn, who has silently been watching me this entire time. I take one of Aryn's hands in both of mine. "I've never been so full or content."

He stares a moment too long before slowly shaking his head and pulling me into his chest. His voice feels like a gentle breeze against my neck. "If you let me, I'll give you a million more of these moments."

"I was only joking." I say this, trying to laugh it off, but my chest feels like someone just dropped a bowling ball on it. I push my face into his shoulder, trying to take even breaths as he runs his hands up and down my back. I push my entire body deeper into him, arms encircling his torso. "I was only joking," I say again, but the way he sighs indicates that we both know I'm lying.

* * *

He continues to hold onto me, quite tightly, for the next few hours. We only separate from one another on two occasions: when the coffee makes its way to my bladder and I have to run to the bathroom, and to get changed. I tried to change back into the dress from last night, but the material felt rough and it didn't seem to sit right in all the places it should. Eventually, without any questions, Aryn lent me a pair of mesh shorts and a tank top, a combination that lets me breathe once again.

"I can't believe we've been laying here for -" He rolls over me to look at the clock. "Three hours. I think I've become part of the mattress."

I groan. "Should we get up? I don't know if I want to get up."

He sidles up to me and gently presses his nose to mine. "How about we take a walk, get some fresh air and exercise?"

I can feel his breath on my lips and it takes all my energy to resist the urge to move just an inch closer. I make a show of stretching, and therefore successfully disentangling myself from him, before hopping out of bed. "You truly are a genius. Let's go!"

Now he groans and stuffs his head under the pillow. "I changed my mind. Come back." He vaguely motions in my direction. I grab his hand and yank, successfully moving him about two inches before giving up. He removes the pillow and smirks at me. "I have perfected dead weight. There is no way you're getting me out of this bed."

I pause, looking around the room. I can't risk getting back into bed with him. "Fine," I shrug, starting to back away. "I'll be going now then. See you at school Monday!"

The minute I turn away from him, I hear him grunting to throw the covers off. He rams into me, chin digging into my shoulder and arms wrapping around my stomach.

He whines into my ear. "Nooo. Please don't leave me."

His heat seeps into me and I involuntarily lean back. Have I ever been this warm before? I don't want to be cold anymore.

"Cold? Are you cold right now?"

My eyes snap open, although I didn't realize I'd shut them. "What do you mean?"

He momentarily lets go of me to turn me around. "You just said you didn't want to be cold anymore. Do you want one of my jackets?"

I pull away from him, arms limp by my side. "I didn't mean to say that out loud." Then I shake my head and start walking away again. "I'm fine."

He whines the entire time we get ready to leave: while I get a glass of water, while we put on our shoes, while we are walking out the door. He only stops when I grab his hand and gently squeeze.

We stop at the edge of the woods. It is quiet again, the only sound the wind rustling the leaves. I suck in a gulp of air, relishing the taste of a sun-infused spring breeze.

"Where exactly should we go?" His voice is carried away on the breeze, too, barely making it to my ears before drifting away again.

"Let's just get lost." I interlock my fingers with his and take a deep breath.

He chuckles, a sound I have become so familiar with. "Have you gotten lost so many times that now it's just a goal of yours?"

I click my tongue. "Never had the opportunity."

"Opportunity? To get lost?"

It sounds so stupid hearing it from someone else. Still, I reply truthfully: "Yes, I haven't been able to travel yet and that's when you get lost. When you're in unfamiliar territory."

"But getting lost isn't a good thing."

Again, he makes sense. That is what most people think so it must be the truth. "Getting lost is a privilege. It means you're going somewhere. If you never get lost, then you are always stuck in the same spot."

"I see..." Suddenly, his grip tightens and his shoulder bumps into mine. "You have such an interesting perspective of the world. I want to see the world like you. I want to get lost, too."

It sounds like he's making fun of me, but when I turn to look at him, he has the softest smile on his face. The type of smile you have when meeting a new-born for the first time, when you recognize all of the potential they have.

"If you could choose anywhere in the world to travel to, where would you pick?"

"Seriously? That's such a tough question." How can I possibly pick one city or country when I've been rooted to one town my entire life? Where would I go if there were no limitations? Where could I go if I let myself dream and got out of my own way? Eventually, I make a choice. "China."

Aryn makes a humming noise in the back of his throat. "Nice choice. But why?"

I shrug, then reconsider. "It's vast in many ways. The landscape, the culture and history. The language is beautiful yet extremely intimidating. But mainly, a photographer could find art every few feet."

"You know, my mother's parents were from China. Hong Kong specifically. They came here in the 70's, had my mom, and the rest is history. I'm sure my mom has photos of their hometowns around the house somewhere if you'd like to see them."

"Oh, that'd be so cool! Have you ever been? Does your mom ever go visit family there?"

He merely shakes his head, lips pursed. Suddenly – because everything is sudden when it comes to him – he stops walking and turns to me. "I never told you how beautiful your photos are. I couldn't stop looking at them that day in your room."

My face instantly heats up. I look at our feet, his torso, the trees surrounding us. Anything to cool myself down. "Thank you. I really appreciate you saying that."

For a brief moment, his thumb traces the outline of my bottom lip. Then we are walking again, my lips pressed together to stop the tingling sensation from spreading.

* * *

"No, seriously! I woke up, in the middle of the night, and Corey was trying to sneak in through my window. My bedroom is on the second floor!"

I double over laughing, my nonexistent abs getting the best workout of their lives. "But wait, wait." I press my hands against my stomach in an effort to stop the pain. "Why was he even there?"

Aryn rolls his eyes, bumping shoulders with me. "He claims he had a nightmare and the only way he could get back to sleep was if I cuddled him. Truly," he smirks now, glancing over at me. "I think he got in trouble with his parents for coming home drunk and he threatened to run away if they grounded him, because he's so dramatic, so he came to my house to scare them."

"But he won't admit that?"

"No, of course not."

I smile softly at him, adoring the way his lips turn up unevenly on both sides. "He really loves you, doesn't he?"

He nods, pauses, and then nods again. "Yeah, we're like brothers. We've been around each other for as long as I can remember and we've always had each other's back." He grips my fingers and tugs until I'm nestled into his side. "He's my platonic soulmate. Don't know what I'd do without him."

We continue throwing questions at one another as we walk, like our favorite foods and what our fears are. Aside from water, I am irrationally scared of spiders and although Aryn isn't scared of heights, he can never convince himself to ride rollercoasters. We avoid talking about our families, an unspoken forbidden topic, although we both know my parents are away more often than not and his father is gone. The details are kept hidden.

My cheek muscles clench and my gut tenses when he speaks; I have never laughed this much. Yet as we continue to walk, I start to question if I'll ruin this. If I continue to let my guard down, if I let Aryn see me vulnerable and shivering, will he end up hating what he sees? I let myself be held by him and think of kissing him. I felt his warmth. I let myself speak, my teeth show. I *enjoyed* being in his bed, in his clothes, in my skin.

Yet that won't last. It never does.

It is an unpredictable and unstoppable force, a darkness so encompassing no pill can sate it, no needle can penetrate it. It sucks the energy right out of me; one day I can be completely content with life and the next I am unable to leave my bed. I know that I should, I want to deep down, but at the moment everything is too bright and too loud. Everything hurts. Not exactly a physical pain, like a pulled muscle or sore back. Not even like a headache. Everything inside of me hurts, like there are splinters extending along the very core of who I am.

I think this to myself and want to suddenly explain it all to Aryn because if I don't show up one day, if I am suddenly just gone, shouldn't he at least know why? Do I at least owe him that? I'm not entirely sure.

I run my tongue along my teeth, mouth brimming with fragments of a reality I'm not sure how to make real yet. Still, I straighten my back and steel myself for polite questions and a refusal to meet my gaze.

I am ready.

Apparently, Aryn is ready, too because he suddenly stops and turns to me. My palm is empty, his grip on my shoulders briefly firm before once again non-existent.

"I like you."

The words are sudden but temporary. Like the burst of fireworks in an almost pitch-black sky.

My tongue, moments ago a friend, is now large and clumsy. "I- yeah... what?"

He nods, takes a deep breath, repeats the firework show. "I like you. Maybe more than I should given the amount of time we've known one another."

Pause. He searches my face and surely, he finds nothing but continues anyway.

"I don't want to have to pretend around you. I don't want you to think of me as something and someone I'm not." He crouches, staring long and hard at the ground beneath him before taking my hands in his. "That's why I want to tell you everything."

I nod, my hands in his, his trust in me. Is he about to show me the skeletons in his closet? Will they become friends with mine? I start to pull myself away from him, but stop and instead ask a question: "Does this have anything to do with you being a monster?"

He pulls away now, walks about ten feet away, comes back to look at my face. Comes back to look me in the eyes. Finally, he groans and throws his head back. "I was barely 14... but I knew what I was doing and that's why I'm a monster."

I expect him to continue but he's silent, back facing me and doubled over. As if he is in pain. As if he can't stand himself.

I walk up to him and place a hand on his back. The reaction is instantaneous. He jerks away from me, both hands balled into fists.

"You don't understand! I did something terrible and I can't ever take it back and it's killing me." His voice gets progressively smaller, like he's receding into himself. An action I am all too familiar with.

I try to get my voice level. "If I don't understand then you have to explain it to me." I try to touch him again, but he backs away. When he speaks, it echoes inside him, trying to fill up all that empty space.

"I killed my father."

My mouth opens on its own accord, only a gush of air

coming out. I stare at him, at his trembling lips, clenched fists, taut neck. His entire body is strung up, tensed and ready to snap.

I know it can't be what it sounds like. Kill is such a strong word, has too many connections with rage and malice. Aryn is scarred, but he still has soft eyes.

I don't know if he's waiting for me to say something. What can I possibly say? I don't know what happened, how it all unfolded. I can't and shouldn't judge his truth, his reality, without hearing his story. The moment I take a step forward, he snaps into action.

"I was so so stupid. A jealous little boy who couldn't get enough attention from his father." He's pacing now, grabbing fistfuls of his hair. "My sister was only 4 but I hated her, Savannah. I hated her because she got all of my father's attention. I know that's so immature but…"

I can hear it now. The tears sliding down his cheeks, echoing into the hollows of his collarbones. He is wheezing, his lungs struggling to pull in the fresh, spring air.

"My father and I got into a fight that day." He holds his hands out before him. "Is it terrible that I can't even remember what we fought about? All I know is that we weren't talking to one another and I got even more pissed because he was praising some crude drawing Allie drew."

He leans against a tree, one hand over his mouth. I see his knees start to buckle but I can't move. He needs to tell me what happened as badly as I need to hear it. He won't let me hold him up. He doesn't believe he deserves it.

"While everyone was asleep," I can't help but hold my breath, not really letting myself believe the worst. "I took that stupid drawing and I lit it on fire. I threw it in the trash can and I walked away." He starts shaking his head, a movement not sufficient enough to demonstrate his disbelief so he begins punching the tree. He continues the story between every few punches. "The whole room caught on fire! My father tried to put it out, but I don't know."

Even from a distance I can see his blood staining the wood. I take a few steps toward him, holding myself so tightly my muscles begin to pulse.

"He inhaled too much smoke. The doctors couldn't do anything. He was in the hospital for months, suffering. And my sister..." He stops mutilating himself, leans against the tree and his blood, and seemingly reaches out to me. "She has burns that will never go away. All because I was some immature 14-year-old who couldn't control his emotions."

I reach out to him, so close I can actually smell the iron from his knuckles. But I don't touch him. I can't bring myself to hold the crying boy. Not until he allows me to.

But I do speak because he needs to hear these words. "It was an accident. You can feel guilty all you want; I'm not telling you not to. And I can't imagine what else you must feel. But you aren't a monster. Aryn," I try to catch his gaze. "It was a tragic accident."

He falls to the ground, legs opened wide in a V and bloody hands out to his sides. His shoulders are shrugging, nostrils flaring. "What do I do?" His whisper strangles me and suddenly, I am between his legs cupping his face.

"You forgive yourself. You become a better person by learning from your mistakes. You become a man your father would be proud of."

He aims his anger at me and I take it. "You didn't know my father."

"I didn't but would he want you to live the rest of your life hating yourself? If he were to see you now, would he think you were happy?" I force him to look at me. I can read the answer in his eyes. "We both know he wouldn't accept you hurting yourself and living in the past. So, what you do now is you forgive, you keep his memory alive, and you move forward."

Once again, I am holding together this broken, fragile boy. I am digesting his reality, all sharp edges and smoky rooms. I saw the fire in him but never thought it'd be burning him from the inside out.

His pain is the tangible, take-your-breath away kind. I want to ease his pain as much as I want to ease mine. Maybe even more. So I brush back his hair, tighten my grip on his still-tense body, and silently promise to help him heal.

Catching Fire

Aryn

She held me like my mother used to. Firm arms, soft breaths.

But it was also different. She wasn't trying to make me forget the nightmares or think only happy thoughts. It was like she grounded me, forced me to look at myself in the mirror and admit what I was feeling. Admit that something terrible happened but that I must still move on with life. I had to at least try.

We just lay there, under the cover of the treetops, for what felt like hours. Our shoulders were glued together, our fingers intertwined. Every so often one of us would gently squeeze the other's hand, as if to say, "I'm here."

The sun eventually begins to dim and Savannah turns into me, just for a moment, before moving away completely. She's shivering.

"Maybe we should go?" She poses it as a question, but it's more of a suggestion. The wind pushes against her as she stands.

"Yeah, it's getting chilly out and I'm starting to get hungry.

Do you want to have dinner at my place?"

Even in the shadows, I can see her eyes brighten and her mouth concave. "Should I?" It's a hesitant yes, a yes that is always used to being a no.

"Of course you should. I'm sure my mother and sister would love to meet you. And be honest, will you eat anything if you go home?"

She doesn't need to answer. I simply grab her hand and we begin the trek back to my house, silhouetted by the moonlight. The leaves crunch beneath our feet, her soft sighs mix with the birds and insects, and I feel completely content.

"Do you think," Savannah begins but pauses, pulling me to a stop. "Do you think your mom will find it strange that I'm in your clothes?" Her eyes widen more each second, her palms sweaty.

I laugh, pulling her along. "Why would she care?"

"Well, you know… I don't want her to think we're sleeping together."

I falter, glad for the darkness descending so she can't see my face explode in a blush. I can't say anything, can only quicken my pace in hopes of leaving my embarrassment behind.

"Not that that would be a bad thing or anything." She tugs on my hand and when I slow my pace, she tucks herself into my side.

I want to tell her that I don't think it'd be a bad thing either, but I'm worried about making her uncomfortable and getting myself too excited. So I squeeze her to me and hope that when we arrive at my house, the red in my cheeks has disappeared.

* * *

I pause at the front door, like I always do, yearning for warm acceptance that's without a doubt within, but that I don't deserve. Savannah, however, sees my hesitation as regret.

Her voice is only a whisper, but it pierces through me. "I can just go home. You don't have to worry about me. I'll be fine. I'm always fine."

My chest constricts as I turn to her and her downcast eyes, muddy puddles wrecked after a storm. I pull her into me, amazed at how natural it feels to have her pressed against me. "I want you here." I pull away and force her to look at me. "You don't have to be alone anymore, okay? You don't always have to be fine."

She grips my shirt, tears pooling in her eyes, before vigorously shaking her head and leaning it against my chest. "Okay."

I grab the door handle and push open the door. We are immediately bombarded by my sister's screams. She is running around in circles in the living room, a towel tied around her shoulders and a pair of my boxers on her head.

I facepalm myself, before turning to apologize to Savannah. But the breath is knocked out of me, like usual around her, because she is smiling. A full-blown smile that lights up her eyes. She turns to me and squeezes my hand before nodding, prodding me to introduce her.

We discard our shoes and I reluctantly let go of her hand. Then I run into the living room, cutting off Allie's route, and pick her up as she continues to scream, this time in surprise.

"Allie, just what do you think you're doing? How much sugar have you had?"

She giggles, tiny feet flapping against any part of me she can reach. "I'm playing a game! I'm a superhero and my power is screaming! It's so powerful that all the villains run away in fear."

I throw her onto the couch, more giggles erupting as she bounces a few times and scrambles back to me. "Well, you're very powerful. But how about we pause the game for now. There's someone I want you to meet."

She's already peeking between my legs, not-so-stealthily staring at Savannah who's standing in the entryway twisting her hands.

"Who is she?" Allie tries to whisper but fails. "Is she your girlfriend?"

I choke on my tongue and try avoiding Savannah's gaze. "Well, uh, she's my friend." It feels wrong saying that because Savannah is so much more. But I don't know what to call her.

Allie gasps, running around my legs and barrels into Savannah. She grips her hand and drags her into the living room. "Sit," Allie demands, coaxing Savannah onto the couch.

Savannah's eyes are as wide as I've ever seen them, but she complies with my sister's demands.

Allie grins at her, bouncing up and down with untapped energy. "What's your name? Do you like my brother? Because he hasn't had a girlfriend in years!"

Savannah covers her mouth, a soft chuckle making its way to my ears. She meets my gaze for only a second. "I'm Savannah," she reaches out to shake Allie's hand. "It's nice to meet you, Allie."

Allie pulls her into a hug. "I'm so glad you're here. I needed someone new to play with because Ry-Ry is boring." She turns to me and sticks out her tongue.

"Hey!" I protest, sitting on the floor in front of them. "That's mean; I can be quite fun to play with. I always play the villain so give me some credit."

Allie just stares at me. "Yeah, but Savannah is prettier than you."

This time, Savannah freely laughs, her eyes crinkling at the edges. She pats Allie on the head. "Thank you. But honestly, you're the prettiest of us all." Savannah relaxes, a visible unbundling of nerves.

"What's all the commotion out here for?"

All three of us turn to the kitchen entryway, where my mom stands with her hands on her hips. Savannah jumps up, fidgets with the hem of my tank top, and glances at me. I simply stand and grab her hand, pulling her over to my mom.

"Mom, this is Savannah. A friend from school and also our neighbor."

My mom's smile engulfs her entire face as she pulls Savannah into yet another hug. I never realized how affectionate my family was. Savannah, although tensing at the physical contacts, lightly wraps her own arms around my mother's frame.

"Savannah! It's been so long, sweetie."

Savannah pulls back, mouth agape. "I'm sorry, do I know you?"

Mom waves her hand dismissively. "It's been such a long time, so perhaps you don't remember me. I mean, your parents and I have both been living here for over 17 years. You and Aryn used to have playdates all the time."

Savannah and I exchange looks, but she doesn't look as surprised as I feel.

"You never told me that."

Mom rolls her eyes, smoothing down the apron around her waist. "You never asked. It's not like I kept it a secret."

I palm my face, confusion growing by the minute. "How

come we stopped hanging out?" I look from my mom to Savannah and back again. Then it clicks: Savannah saying she knew me, that she had a picture of me. Does she remember us hanging out when we were little and if she does, why hasn't she told me?

Mom sighs, reaching out as if she wants to touch Savannah, but last minute decides against it. Instead, she gently strokes the necklace around Savannah's neck, an accessory I learned she rarely takes off. "My husband gave this to you for your 5th birthday. I doubt you remember."

Now Savannah looks confused as she grips the silver chain. "He did? This is my favorite necklace. I don't remember ever being without it."

"You were obsessed with ribbons so when he found this, he knew you would love it." My mom's eyes droop, like she's remembering something she wishes she didn't have to. "Turns out he was right." Then she turns to me and shrugs, as if my question is just now reaching her. "I don't know, honey. Life just got in the way, I suppose." I can tell she doesn't want to say anymore.

Suddenly she claps, a ringing noise echoing through the house. "Dinner is almost ready. Are you staying?" She gently grabs Savannah's hands, as if the touch would break her. Hell, maybe it would.

Savannah gulps and then nods. I notice her squeezing my mom's hand in response. "I would love that."

Mom's hands run over Savannah's hair on both sides, a gentle stroking motion that somehow even calms me. "I'm so glad."

* * *

170

Dinner at my house has never been so animated. Yes, it's always been noisy, but today there is so much laughter my sides begin to ache. I can't help but steal glances at Savannah the entire time, completely enamored by her bright eyes and wide grins. I've never seen her so open, so vulnerable. It puts my heart into overdrive.

"Savannah, sweetie, would you like more potatoes?" My mom holds the bowl toward Savannah, but she shakes her head. "Please help yourself, you haven't eaten much."

Savannah presses her lips together but shakes her head again. "Thank you, Mrs. Cooper, but I'm already so full."

My mom frowns, eyeing Savannah's plate which is still half full. We've been eating for over 15 minutes and Savannah has only taken a few forkfuls, mainly moving food around. "Alright, that's fine." Her smile returns. "And please call me Jia."

I can see Savannah mouthing my mother's name before returning the smile.

"So, Savannah, how is junior year going for you?"

Small talk. I should've known this was unavoidable.

Savannah tilts her head to the side. "Uhm, you know, it's going okay. Can't complain too much, teachers are nice." She shrugs.

"Do you know what colleges you're going to apply for next fall?"

"Mom!" I hiss, glaring at her. She holds her hands up defensively.

"Well," Savannah coughs into her arm. "I don't think I've given it much thought. I think my goal has always been simply to graduate and then I could-" She purses her lips, either thinking of an answer or stopping herself from saying something. "Then I'd figure it out."

My mom lowers her eyes, slowly nodding her head as if something's clicking in her mind. Savannah watches her, panic on her face.

"But!" She says suddenly, eyes nervous. "I'm interested in photography. I just need to do more research about making that into a career."

Allie, who has been quiet up until this point, bangs on the table. "Can you take my picture? I want to be a model!"

Savannah giggles and nods, reaching over to ruffle her hair.

"I think that's a great profession, dear." My mom says, donning a sad smile. I don't know why and now is not the time to ask.

"Your pictures are amazing, Sav. I'm sure you'll become so famous that you'll forget all about us little people." I chuckle, but it gets stuck in my throat when she examines my face.

"Never," she breathes, lingering a moment longer before bringing a forkful of food to her mouth.

* * *

When everyone has finished eating, I help my mom bring the dirty dishes into the kitchen as Allie once again claims all of Savannah's attention.

I touch my mom's arm, gaining her attention. "Thank you for letting her stay for dinner. I... you know, her house..." I rub the back of my neck, not really sure what I'm trying to say.

Mom touches my cheek, a soft smile directed solely at me. "Honey, I know." I lean into her touch. It's been so long. Too long. And it's all my fault. "It's so nice seeing her again. She's grown into a beautiful young woman, hasn't she?" She winks at me before turning back to dishes, letting them soak under the hot water.

"Mom, what really happened when we were younger? How come I don't remember her?"

Mom tenses, slightly shaking her head. "It was so long ago. You were too young to remember anyway."

"Is it because she drowned?"

"So she told you about that, yeah?" I nod as she turns around to face me, hands dripping with soap. "That's what started it all, I think. Everything just turned sour after that. I mean, of course she was traumatized. But her parents..." She blows air out of her cheeks, turns off the water, and dries her hands. "Aryn... it's complicated. She's... she's not well."

I shake my head, eyes furrowing. "What do you mean? She didn't say she felt sick today."

"No, I mean, it's complicated." She repeats, twisting the dish towel in her hand. "Did you know her parents basically just up and left a few years ago? I still see her mom, Sarah, occasionally, at the grocery store or somewhere else in town. But Savannah's never with her. Her dad, I think he just left."

"Why? Why would he leave them?"

"I imagine it's pretty traumatic to see your child die. I don't think he could handle the fact that they weren't there to protect her. I'm sure there's more to it, but I don't have all the answers. I wish I did."

I take a deep breath, processing the information even though it isn't much. My legs want to buckle. Too many questions are running through my head.

"I don't know if you want to hear this," she starts, patting the top of my left hand. "But I think you need to know how serious this was and could get." She waits for me to look at her before continuing. "I went over to their house a few years ago, just to check in and hopefully catch up. I knocked and knocked and although Sarah's car wasn't there, I knew someone was home." She looks up at me, tears brimming but refusing to fall. "I knew something was wrong. The door was unlocked so I just walked in and she... she was just lying there. Barely breathing."

I don't know if my face shows the shock running through my body, but it feels like someone just lit a match along my veins. I look at Savannah in the living room, her soft smile, her guarded eyes, and wonder what the hell she's been through.

"I took her to the hospital. At first, they wouldn't let me stay with her, but they couldn't even get a hold of her parents. All they told me was that she was severely malnourished and needed to stay in the hospital for a few days."

Her breath stutters, hand gripping mine just a little tighter. "I don't know what happened after that, if her parents came back. I don't know what's happened in the past few years. I honestly didn't even know they still owned the house." She looks past me, hands slipping away. "I should've checked in on her more often, but..."

I know she's thinking of dad, of how sick she got after his death. She had to take care of herself at that time. And us. She can't feel guilty about not taking care of others, as well.

"She looks better now. Happier, especially when looking at you. Just..." She takes my face into her hands and looks me dead in the face. "Don't break her heart, do you hear me? She may look tough, but she's broken in places we can't see."

I swallow my tears and lean against her, my heart thrumming against my ear drums. Her palm runs up and down my back a few times and I allow myself to breathe, to relax against my mother like when I was a child. "I won't, mom. I promise."

* * *

My entire body hums in anticipation as I wait for Savannah. Allie practically begged Savannah to take her to bed, her doe eyes making it near impossible to say no. So, I'm waiting on the edge of my bed for her, straining to hear their hushed whispers and traded secrets. My fingers get tangled in my bed sheets, my grip getting tighter and tighter as the minutes tick by until they ache. I examine the dried blood caked into my knuckles, my poor attempt at cleaning myself up doing nothing to hide the most recent physical proof of the damage I inflict on myself. I ball my hands into fists and hiss, torn between wanting to ask her questions I haven't properly formulated yet and wanting to merely spend the rest of the night in the bubble of normalcy we created.

It's almost as if she knows I'm in pain and conflicted because she's suddenly at the door, a small arch in her brows.

She whispers, "Aryn," but it seems like a scream. I've never loved my name as much as I do at this moment. "Let's go to the bathroom."

Without question, I pathetically follow her across the hall where she wordlessly closes the door behind us and pushes me against the sink.

"Allie is already asleep?" I question, trying to catch her eye.

"Yes, she tired herself out by asking me a million questions. Then she asked me to tell her a story, so I panicked and told her how we met." She chuckles, running a washcloth under the facet until it's damp, the hot water steaming up the mirror.

175

"You remember how we met? I thought you were basically sleep-walking and wouldn't recall our conversation at all."

She places the damp washcloth on my knuckles without warning and I flinch against the heat. "Of course I remember." She continues to dab against my red and fraying skin in silence and the ball in my throat prevents me from saying anything else.

After wetting the cloth again, she wrings it out and lays it on the counter. She points to the cabinet, "Do you have peroxide in there?" I merely nod and she opens it, taking out the peroxide and a bag of cotton balls.

"I hope it doesn't sting."

She scoffs, soaking a cotton ball and spreading my palm on the bathroom counter. "Don't be such a baby. If you don't want the medicine to hurt you, maybe you shouldn't be so reckless in the first place."

I snatch my hand away, my anger sudden and hot. "You don't know anything. Don't judge what I do; you have no idea how I feel." I attempt to grab the cotton ball from her. "Let me do it."

She sighs and leans against the counter. Then she pins me with a stare, one devoid of any emotion. Or maybe an emotion I can't quite identify. "Stop." She reaches for my hand again and grips it firmly. "Just let me help."

I bare my teeth when she presses it against my skin, but it tingles more than it stings. I stare at her hands as she daps my knuckles dry.

"No band aids for you. Let the cuts breathe." She pulls my hands into hers and finally looks at me. "Just don't get blood on me during the night."

I can't say anything. I don't know how I would even muster the courage to say the words if I found them. Her eyes pin me, simultaneously telling me that no, she doesn't know how I feel, but that she's already proven herself a worthy listener.

In a daze I'm led back to my room. Savannah orders me to close my eyes as she changes back into the pajamas I lent her the previous night and even though I squeeze my eyes shut so tightly they hurt, my entire body heats up.

"Are you tired?" The bed dips as she squirms her way under the covers, back pressed against the wall. "My body feels exhausted but I'm also extremely restless."

I climb in next to her, crossing my legs beneath me in hopes of hiding my jitteriness. "I can stay up for a while."

She hums in response, hugging my pillow to her chest. "Allie is a firecracker. I forgot what it's like being around kids." She smiles into the pillow. "And your mom, wow." She locks eyes with me. "It feels like I've known her forever. She's so warm, like a cup of hot cocoa on a cold winter day." This time she laughs, a small blush spreading across her cheeks.

I reposition myself so I can face her. "Savannah, last night you said something..." I make sure she's still looking at me. "You said you knew me and that I was the boy in the picture. What does that mean?"

She looks away from me. "I'd have to show you. It's not easy to explain. I will show you when it's time, okay? I promise."

I want to pry some more, but I merely nod. I want to hear her speak as much as I want to feel her skin against mine and my pinky twitches.

She turns to me and smiles, but it doesn't reach her eyes, not like earlier. We stare at each other for a moment longer, my body heating up, before she closes her eyes. "Aryn, why does your house feel like this?"

I tilt my head to the side, wondering if she's referring to the temperature. "Feel like what?"

She clenches the pillow tighter against her chest. "Like a home."

"Ah…" All the air releases out of me. How can I possibly answer that without reminding her that her house lacks all the elements of a loving home? How can I possibly rub the fullness of my family in her face, when all she's used to is empty walls? "I don't know, Sav. My mom tries to make sure it's as homey as possible, whatever that means. Especially since my dad passed away."

She turns onto her back, eyes tracing the same ceiling that I do every morning and every night. She nods but doesn't say anything for a while. Then she turns to me, eyes bright with a pain I've never seen on her face, on anyone's face. Her eyes are flooding, tears streaming down her cheeks and she hiccups. "Is it my fault?"

I don't think. My hands just immediately reach for her. But she recoils and props herself up in the bed. "Is it my fault they don't love me? Do I deserve to… to constantly feel like I'm drowning? Will I always be this shell of a person?" She hiccups again, tears still flowing freely from her eyes even as she attempts to wipe them, attempts to halt their progress by tipping her head back and blinking.

"Savannah…" That's all I can say. I don't think she's necessarily waiting for me to speak. I think she's hoping I'll simply listen.

She palms her chest. "Oh god, I can't even stop crying." She laughs, an empty sound that hurts my ears. "You don't understand. No one understands and I don't know how to explain. When I try," she waves her hands in front of her, like she's trying to locate the words in the air. "No one listens anyway."

"Hey, hey." I stop her hands mid-air. "I'm listening. I'm here for you, just like you've been there for me." She gulps, nods. "What do you feel?"

A pause, a look of panic. "Too little. Too much." She narrows her eyes and pulls her hands from mine. She holds herself. "That day, when you said I was dead inside, that we're both dead inside... You were right. But-" Her arms tighten, her frame shakes. Then she's leaning across the bed, into me, and silently begging me to hold her instead. "It's more than that. I feel nothing at all or everything all at once. I just want... I want to be okay."

I pull her into me, trying to soak up all the tears, somehow fuse both our pain together. Her pain becomes mine. My pain becomes hers. She shudders against me, bones sharp as a blade and digging into every soft spot.

She curls her face into my neck. Her breath is warm, staggering. "I want to wake up and know that I'm alive."

I grip her face in my hands, softly pressing my fingers into her skin. "Do you feel this?" She gulps, refusing to open her eyes. But she nods. "You can feel me and I'm real. I'm here," I take her hand and place it on my chest. Over my furiously beating heart. "I'm alive, so you are, too."

She nods, slowly opening her eyes. She blinks repeatedly, blinded by her own tears. But I can tell when she sees me, when she feels my heart beating right out of my chest.

There are words dangling on the tip of my tongue, but it's not the time nor the place. I want to bare my heart to her, illogically and recklessly, but I can't. I know she doesn't feel the same. Suddenly, though, she reels me in.

"I have a question." She holds my gaze, palm still pressed

against my chest, which is heaving as if I've just run a marathon.

"Yeah, you can ask me anything."

She bites her lip and my eyes follow the movement before I can stop myself. "Will you kiss me?"

My eyes snap back up to hers and my chest is smoking. "W-what? I mean… Are you sure?"

Her fingers take hold of my shirt, bracing herself or pulling me closer, I have no clue. "I want to feel how real you are."

I nod to disguise my gulp and I have to wipe my clammy hands on my pants. We both move forward, seconds seeming to last minutes before we're finally nose to nose.

I cup her cheek, wanting nothing more than to close the remaining distance. "Sav, are you sure about this?"

She takes in a shaky breath, her grip on my shirt tightening, and her breath flutters against my lips. Just as I move my hand behind her neck, she's kissing me and all the air is knocked right out of me.

Everything inside me burns and it is slow, delicious. She somehow still tastes like blueberries and her lips are so soft. They slant over mine like we've done this a million times. The kiss is gentle yet terrifying. It is real.

The whole room catches fire.

Alone Again

Savannah

The throbbing in my head intensifies as I move through the halls, a side effect of two hours of sleep and endless rampant thoughts running through my head during the night. My lips still tingle from the feeling of his pressing against mine, tiny little shocks that make my mouth feel numb. The kiss lingered; his lips chapped but soft, molding against mine in an urgent manner like we could only breathe if breathing into one another. It was dizzying and I had to grip him tighter to me because I felt my body tremble even though I was sitting. But it all ended too quickly and I was reeling afterward, eyes fluttering closed and snapping open as he drifted off beside me.

My eyes dart back and forth, trying to catch a glimpse of him. But as I move forward, my brain slams against my skull and my heart grows wings, flapping against my chest, panicked. Trapped. I pause at my locker, fingers shaking as I twist the lock. Then I'm rummaging through the metal compartment, grasping a small pill bottle and twisting the cap off.

As I bring the pill to my mouth, Bailey appears out of nowhere. Her eyes follow my hand as I pop the pill and swallow it dry, wishing I had some water to moisten my dry throat.

"What the hell did you just take?" She spits the words at me and I shrug.

"My medicine. Why?"

She pries the bottle from my palm and examines it. "Savannah, this is an old prescription. You were supposed to stop taking this months ago." She opens her backpack and shoves the bottle inside, pills rattling. "Do you not have the new prescription? Your mom was supposed to give it to you when she came to visit."

I slowly close my locker, trying to wrack my brain for any forgotten information. "No, I don't remember her mentioning anything." I gather cheek fulls of saliva and swallow it back down, hoping the pill stays where it belongs.

"For fucks sake." She passes a hand over her face and sighs. Then, just as suddenly as she appeared, she grabs my arm, "Do you have any idea how sick you can get if you take this type of medicine on an empty stomach? The side effects are already brutal as is, but you not eating doesn't help."

I shrug in response, my arm throbbing beneath her grip. "You're hurting me."

Bailey blinks and then pulls her hand back like she's been burned. "I-I'm sorry, Sav. I just..." She readjusts the strap of her messenger bag. "This is all so stressful. There are too many moving pieces all the damn time. I can't keep track of anything."

I take a step back and my face heats up. "I'll do it. I don't need to be managed anymore."

Bailey merely stares at me, lips forming one straight, thin

line. Then her body comes alive and she tries to reach out for me, but I can't stand the thought of her skin on mine, so I lean back.

"You're right," I admit, trying to keep my voice flat. "This is all too stressful. I'm too much. You aren't my caregiver so don't worry about it anymore."

"No, wait, Savannah. That's not what I meant!"

I can't will myself to move, but I feel like I'm in constant motion. I meet her gaze and hold it. "You know, I'm tired of all this, too."

It must've been how stoic my face was or perhaps it was the even tone of my voice because Bailey suddenly looks as if she's seen a ghost.

"Sav, I-I don't... please don't tell me...."

I feel the rage sprout from my fingertips at her inability to say it. "No, Bailey. God dammit. Why do you all think I'm going to just go kill myself? Is that what you want?"

Bailey's eyes widen and I have to remind myself that we're in the hallway, without a shred of privacy. I step closer to her so that I don't have to scream, but as her eyes shift to look over my shoulder, I realize it's far too late for hushed conversation. When I turn, my gut twists into knots. Aryn stares at me, eyes glazed with confusion and hurt. He stares at me as if he's trying to unravel all the secrets of the universe, all the secrets within me. It makes me want to puke.

In one hand he's holding a muffin, littered with little blue specks, and in the other he's holding a fist. But when I fully turn towards him, he drops both and displays his palms. Like he's trying to make room for me. Like he's trying to show me he won't cause any further damage. But then he opens his mouth and I wish he didn't.

"You-you want to die? I- how come..." He gulps, his open palms now shaking. "Why didn't you tell me how bad it was?" His voice is soft, but I can hear the hurt rolling off his tongue. The anger. And his anger fuels my own.

Just like his hands, my body is trembling. The headache I tried nursing is back full force and my stomach churns like I've just digested acid. When I speak, my voice tears out of me. "I don't owe you anything."

I don't know what I expected his reaction to be. But I definitely didn't expect him to stumble backwards, like my fist just found a home in his gut. Like I just tore his heart directly from his chest and stomped on it. But that's how he reacts and my fingers tingle with the urge to reach out to him, to mend the wounds I'm creating even though no one can see them but us.

How did we end up like this when just the other day we blended into one another? How can I hurt others when I know how consuming pain is?

I blink away tears, wanting to both laugh at how dramatic this is and scream at how nothing can ever seem to stay right. I ruin everything I touch.

But Aryn suddenly recoils, eyes narrowing in on me, a certain softness to the crinkles around his eyes. He steps forward, palms once again laid bare for me, and before I know it, I'm leaning into his chest. "Let me in," he whispers against my hair, fingers digging into my hips like I'll disappear at any moment. And I might; the urge is there. Instead, I find myself nodding against his shoulder, sucking in a breath I wasn't aware I was holding.

I can do this. I can let him in, let him see the scars carved deep within me. Let him smell the blood that taints my fingertips. I can let him in. I want to let him in.

But I'm convinced the universe is conspiring against me because the moment I let myself sink into the softness of his body, I'm pulled back to reality. Back to the school halls, back to expired pills, back to the urge to flee. But it's *her* that has this façade crashing down around us. I never thought she'd come back, looking for the boy she once had claws dug so deep into.

"Aryn, baby," Clara coos, heels rapidly tapping against the tiled floor.

I'm out of Aryn's arms now, though he tries to reattach himself to me. I push myself into the metal lockers, watching as this creature in human skin drags her nails down Aryn's forearm. He doesn't even move; I can feel how stiff he is beside me.

Clara barely glances at me, ignoring me on purpose. "Aryn, how come you haven't texted me back? We need to choose a color scheme for the dance. I'm thinking pink, but like rose pink, not salmon."

I must make a noise in the back of my throat because both of their eyes snap to me. Aryn finally comes to his senses and pushes Clara off of him, moving to the other side of me against the lockers. I'm a barrier, his protector.

"What the hell are you going on about?" Although his voice comes out laced in acid, I feel his arm twitch beside me. He's scared and I don't know why.

Clara's eyes slowly travel from his face to mine and rage is once again at my fingertips. I don't like her eyes lingering on him like he's prey, like he's just a slab of meat.

"You're taking me to the spring dance." It's not a question. "I took you to my sophomore spring formal, and now you should return the favor and take me to your junior one. Unless…" She stares at me, a slight smirk on her heavily lip-glossed mouth. But her smirk slips as I refuse to look away.

She laughs, "Please don't tell me you're with this beast now?" She moves toward him, but I place myself in front of him, his breath tickling the back of my neck. "This is crazy, Aryn." She tries to make eye contact with him over my shoulder. "What? Are you suddenly too good for me? Or is she helping you forget like I did?"

Aryn grunts behind me, fingers finding their way to my shirt and clutching. I lean back slightly, his warm chest flat against my back. There is a small crowd around us now, Jacklyn and Corey joining the ranks beside Bailey, who without a doubt texted the former. Corey's face is beet red, fists curled into tight balls. I'm so confused my head begins spinning.

Clara examines her nails with a smile so sinister she could be a horror movie villain. "I see, so that's what this is. You're fucking her to forget dear old dad, yeah?" Aryn grips me tighter. "Can't say I'm surprised. But really, her? I would've come if you called. You can't forget that you're mine, Aryn."

My jaw ticks and suddenly everything comes crashing down around me. The pain, the fear, the rage. The image of Aryn kissing me fights with the image of his mouth on hers, his skin touching hers. I can't even process my movements, but Aryn tugs on my shirt and I see Bailey take a step forward. But they're too late.

I can't help but smile as blood spurts from Clara's nose, my knuckles throbbing from the impact. I know I should feel bad but god, hitting her and hearing her whimper feels so good. It makes the pain in my chest lessen. I take a deep breath through my nose, hoping the anger is gone but when I open my mouth, my words quicker than my brain, I know the anger isn't gone yet. Blood wasn't enough.

"You stay away from him. If I see you so much as look at him, I swear to god you'll need a whole new face." I was letting the words slip forcefully but quietly through my lips, but now I'm screaming. "He's not yours! He never was!"

Clara stares up at me, hands covered in her own blood, narrowed eyes filled with tears. I don't know when she fell to the floor, but she belongs there. "You're crazy, you bitch! You're going to regret this." As she scrambles to her feet, heels stumbling to support her, I merely smile.

"Try me, I have nothing to lose."

I watch her walk away and then I'm gasping for air, pulling my arms tight around me as the eyes in the crowd stare and their mouths murmur. I was invisible and now they all see me. See what I've done, what I've let myself become.

The darkness. I let the darkness in and I liked it.

I back myself into the lockers and flinch when Aryn tries to touch me, turn away when Bailey does the same. They're all speaking at me, tongues pushing out words that won't fix anything. That won't fix me.

When the crowd has cleared and all that's left is the five of us, I burst out of my skin. I want to scream but the only thing that comes out of my mouth is bile and I make it to the trash just in time. Bailey runs a hand up and down my back, but it only makes me feel worse.

I wipe my mouth and turn to them. Corey is speaking into Aryn's ear, who is in turn staring at me. I can't decipher the look in his eyes, but I can only imagine what's running through his head. Bailey and Jacklyn simultaneously try to reach for me, but I just shake my head and reach for my bag. I can't look at any of them, but I know. I know they are disgusted. I'm disgusted.

"I'm sorry. I'm so sorry." The tears come quickly, but before any of them can say anything, my legs carry me down the hall and out the doors. But even then I can't breathe.

* * *

My limbs are heavy the next morning and it takes me more mental energy to get out of bed than it does physical energy. I scrub myself red and raw in the shower and I tug itchy fabric over my skin, but even so, I stand rooted to the spot as I try to convince myself to open the front door. I can't bring myself to turn the knob, can't stomach the thought of stepping outside and facing all of them. I grip the straps of my bookbag and gulp, knowing that if I were to leave, I'd be nothing more than a shell for the rest of the day. I won't be able to pretend. So what's the point?

I strip until I'm nothing more than bare skin and goose-bumps and slither back into my bed. The cold sheets feel good. I feel safe and for the next few days, although it feels like mere hours, I stay in these sheets because I'm scared to go anywhere else.

The girls come by every day and try convincing me to come out, to come to school, to eat. But I can only manage to grunt in response, so they know I'm alive and breathing. But not alive and well. I'm proud of myself for remembering to lock my bedroom door, otherwise they would've barged in and forced me to move, to feel. But I can't. I'm not ready. I'm too caught up in hating myself and the world. Too caught up in the thoughts that leave me breathless.

I keep my phone charged, just in case I feel the urge to hurt myself. Right now, I don't have the energy to and perhaps that's the only reason I haven't grabbed the switchblade hidden beneath my mattress. As long as I stay still, nothing hurts. As long as I don't think, I don't feel.

I sleep more in these few days than I have in the past few months and it works wonders for my body. But I can't stomach much food and have only managed to drink two water bottles in however long I've holed myself up for and I know it's not enough; my mouth is dry and my throat hurts when I swallow. But it's a pain I can endure.

Aryn calls me every day, three to four times, but he never leaves a voicemail. I wish he did. I miss his voice, but I can't bring myself to call him. What could I possibly say?

I check my phone, the calendar informing me it's early Thursday and I heave a sigh. I force my limbs from under the sheets and drag myself to the bathroom. I avoid the mirror. That girl in the reflection will only make me feel worse.

The hot water burns and I scrub the sweat that's accumulated off my skin until it's once again red and raw. I pull out clumps of hair, the knots refusing to loosen their grip unless I use brute force. Once I feel like I've successfully crawled my way through the pits of hell, I hobble back into my room in time to hear my phone go off again. I sigh, feeling somewhat defeated. Not bothering to check who's calling, I breathe a greeting into it.

"Yes?"

"Oh!" His voice immediately sends chills down my spine, though I don't miss the shock lacing it. "You answered. I didn't expect you to answer..." He trails off and then clears his throat. "I've been calling and calling and you never answered and honestly, I thought the worst and I don't even really know what to say because there's too much I need to say but I-"

"Hey," I interrupt him, his rambling cute but tangential. My voice comes out as a salve and I hear him take a shuddering breath. "Are you okay?"

There is a deafening silence before a laugh, gruff and unexpected, comes from his end.

"You're not seriously asking me that, are you? Do you know how worried I've been about you these past few days? Are *you* okay?" Aryn takes a deep breath and before I can even formulate a response, before I can decide if I feel fine enough to say yes, I am okay, he continues, "Because I miss you and I would really like to see you."

I sigh, resisting the urge to curl into a ball full of nerves and confusion. Instead, I settle on the edge of my bed, only now noticing the endless stream of water dripping from my hair. "I don't know... I don't really want to see anyone right now. I-I don't know what I'd say."

He shuffles, then heaves a sigh against the speaker. "Is it something I did? Please let me know if I somehow scared you away and how I can fix it." It's barely there but his voice cracks and my heart heaves against my chest. I go to respond; I want to placate his fears more than I want to soothe my own. But he's not done. "And the thing- the thing with Clara, that was complete bullshit. There's nothing between the two of us. Please believe me. You have to believe me, Savannah."

"Aryn," it's a whisper, a barely-there plea, but he hears me and goes quiet. "I believe you. I do. And I..." I swallow the hesitation, pull the towel tighter around me as if that small movement could hold me together. "I miss you, too."

His voice remains quiet as he issues his own plea. "Then

come see me. I don't know how much longer I can go without seeing you." He waits for me to answer, but I can't find the words. "Come to me."

I press my palm against my eye and grip my phone so tightly it begins to hurt. "I can't. I'm sorry, but I just can't."

* * *

Aryn's voice rings in my ear throughout the day and it's the only thing keeping me sane. Until I see lightning streak across the sky, and I can't help but grip the sheets. It's followed closely by thunder and the onslaught of rain is terrifying, savage. I peek behind my curtains but can't see out the window, the thick blanket of rain hiding the entire forest from me. It only takes a moment for the panic to set in.

Before I can even process my movements, I'm running out of my bedroom and down the stairs. I slip halfway down, falling forward and barely catching myself against the wall. I right myself, basically sliding the rest of the way down on my butt and slip on my sneakers. I pause only briefly to examine my attire; a camisole, sleep shorts, lots of skin. I should at least put on a hoodie to buffer the raging wind. But no, the longer I wait, the more likely it is that he'll be gone. And then what?

I burst out the front door, immediately being pelted with rain that honestly feels like hail. Thunder roars around me and as I run into the thicket of trees, I slip again, this time onto my ass and into a mud puddle that's growing by the second. Again, I pull myself up and pump my legs, trying to dodge puddles but stumbling the entire way. I know this path like the back of my hand, but the wind is blowing me everywhere and the rain just won't stop. I fall to my knees and gasp for air. Or maybe

I'm screaming, or wailing, I have no clue. I look everywhere, I dig my hands into the soil, which is now mostly water and I come up with mud, with earth.

He's nowhere to be seen.

I know for a fact I'm crying now and I convince myself to push forward, toward the house on the other side of the dark, dark woods. Even though my eyes are clouded by both tears and rain, I can see the light. I can see him waiting for me.

At least that's what I'm hoping for.

Alive

Aryn

It felt like someone punched me right in the solar plexus. Like I couldn't breathe, like my body refused to function properly.

All because of her. Because the need to see her and touch her again was so overwhelming. Because her wanting to see me, but refusing to, made me feel like both the luckiest and most cursed creature on earth.

I'm still thinking about her hours later at the dinner table. Allie is slowly shoveling peas into her mouth, eyelids drooping every few seconds and then snapping back up. Mom's head is turned slightly in her direction but she isn't concerned enough to put her to bed just yet. But when the first roar of thunder screams above us, Allie shrieks, her peas going everywhere and her eyes widening. She's definitely not going to bed anytime soon now.

The thunder is followed by an eerie quiet, disrupted only by streaks of lightning that discolor the entire room. The lights flicker but stay bright. I'm so distracted by Allie's whines, the roaring thunder, and my own thoughts, that it takes me a moment to recognize the chime of the doorbell.

I scooch my chair back and share a quizzical look with my mom. Who the hell—?

As I wrench the door open, I lose all train of thought. Savannah is standing there, looking like she just waged war with nature. She's completely drenched and barely covered. Once again, she's all skin and cotton, but this time she's shivering, knees knocking against one another. She peers at me beneath her hair, which is plastered against her cheeks, forehead, and neck. If it were anyone else, they'd look like a drowned rat. But she fails to look like anything but a fierce lion, albeit a very wet one.

I stare for a moment longer before coming to my senses; there's a fucking storm raging outside. "Savannah, what the hell are you doing outside?" I reach for her, but she flinches and shakes her head. "Sav, get inside. You're going to get sick."

"I can't," she whispers, her voice scratchy and pleading. She meets my gaze and the floodgates release. "Aryn, I can't find him. Everything is flooded and I kept searching but it's hard to see, but I know that he has to be out there somewhere. I have to find him, okay? I- you have to help me otherwise I don't know." She shakes her head.

As I take in the mud under her fingernails, it suddenly clicks. "Sav, you went looking for your tulip in this type of weather?" I reach out for her again and she lets me run my hand down her arm, slick from the rain, all the way to her hand. I tug, barely a pull, and she's burying her face in my chest.

"Aryn!" My mom screeches from the kitchen, making both Savannah and I jump. "Are you trying to let the storm in?"

Before Savannah can resist, I pull her further into the house and slam the door shut, locking it behind us. "Stay here for just a moment," I tell her, only moving away when she nods.

I rush into the kitchen. "Mom, where is that flower I brought in the other day?" She merely looks at me like I've grown two heads. "It's important. I need it, now."

She opens her mouth, but then must decide it's too much effort to grill me. She rubs a palm down Allie's back and gestures to the fridge with her head.

I let out a huge sigh when I see the recently potted tulip. Her tulip. I take it down from the top of the fridge and shoot my mom an appreciative smile before making my way back to Savannah. She must not hear me coming because when I clear my throat, she jumps again. Her eyes dart from me to the flower with furrowed brows until settling on me.

"You-you took him? I- how did- what?" Her eyes are wide and even beneath all the watery mud, her face flushes.

I hand her the pot, which she quickly hugs to her chest. "I knew the storm was going to get rough, so I went out early yesterday and dug it up. I knew you'd be devastated if it, uh... if he died."

She silently stares at the pot for a moment before gently placing it down on the table by the front door. She shivers, turning to me with emotions dancing in her eyes that I can't possibly decipher. Finally, after what feels like hours of her tracing my face, she speaks.

"Why?"

I have no clue what she's asking. "Why did I pot the tulip for you?"

She shakes her head, wet curls slapping against her skin. "Why do you care so much about me? Especially after what I did on Monday."

I laugh and, without really even thinking, grab her face in my hands. "You protected me, which you seem to do a lot of, and that only made me care more about you." She opens her mouth, but I continue. "You feel bad about drawing a little blood, but who cares? Clara deserved it and you shouldn't be punishing yourself for that." I lean down to make sure she's looking at me. "You shouldn't be punishing yourself at all. I know I'm not one to talk, but you need to realize that you're amazing and I'm not going to let you go over something as trivial as breaking my ex's nose. I don't know if there's anything that could drive me away from you and that's terrifying as shit but-"

"I love you."

Those three words halt everything and cause a ripple effect. She says them with such conviction, no hesitation at all, that I lose my breath, my balance. I don't mean to, but I pull myself away from her, so I can breathe, so I can relish the way those words feel against my skin. I allow myself to openly soak in every feature of her face, to tell myself that it's okay if I say it back. But I take too long. I'm quiet for too long, because her face falls, lips quivering.

"No, Sav, I-" Allie begins singing from the kitchen, basically shouting, and I lose my concentration. Savannah moves toward the door, but I grab her wrist and begin dragging her up the stairs.

"Aryn, wait!" She digs her heels into the carpet, but I won't let her leave. Never again. Not when I have so much to say. She quickly slips off her sneakers before stumbling after me.

I only release her when we make it to the bathroom, making sure to lock it behind us. She glares at me and I can see all the curses she's thinking of hurling at me fighting to leave her mouth. But I claim it before she can say anything.

She freezes when I kiss her, no doubt eyes wide and wet.

Her fingers grip my shirt briefly before she's pulling away.

"Aryn, plea-"

"I love you," I whisper it against her mouth, but it's firm. Firm enough to silence her, firm enough to make her go soft against me. I place my cheek against hers. "I love you even though we're both such a mess." I suck in a breath and she breathes with me. "I think I've loved you since the first day I saw you."

Her palm is soft against my chest, but I move back anyway. Her eyes are brimming with tears and I wipe my thumb beneath one of them, catching droplets as they fall.

She hiccups. "How can you love me when I'm so fucked up?"

I can't help but laugh, taking her hands in mine and squeezing. "I could ask you the same thing."

She leans in, shivers against me, and knocks her head against my chest. "You have to know you drive me crazy."

"Again, I can say the same thing about you." I run my hands up and down her arms a few times before realizing her shivers won't go away. "Let's get you warmed up." Reluctantly, I pull away, much to her displeasure, too, because a little whine erupts from the back of her throat. My heart quite literally melts and I can't help but let out my own sound of protest, but I chuckle to cover it up and turn on the shower.

To my surprise, Savannah steps right into the shower, clothes and all, and sighs as she leans against the tiles. She looks down at her bare feet and giggles. "I'm covered in so much dirt. How could you even kiss me when I'm wearing half the forest?"

I pause for just a moment, but think fuck it and step into the shower, as well. I push her from under the shower and against the tiles. She stares up at me, brown eyes melting under my stare. I cup her face, trail my fingers down her neck and then lose them in her hair. "You're beautiful. No matter what you tell yourself, you'll always be beautiful to me. Absolutely and undeniably."

She gulps, hard, and brushes her hand against my cheek before letting it fall to my chest and then to my hip. I'm stiff, everywhere, and I try to shift so I'm not pressed against her, but she lets out a breath and I know she feels me. Her hand is shaky as she slides it under my shirt and suddenly, I'm bright red.

"I-I don't have a six pack." I stammer, suddenly nervous that she won't find me attractive stripped bare. That I'm not her type physically.

She pauses, eyes snapping to mine and trailing over my face. Then she bursts out laughing - a full-on guttural laugh that eases all the tension in my chest. She continues to lift my shift and before I know it, I'm shirtless. Both her hands are on me now and I feel little shocks everywhere the pads of her fingers press. She leans forward and only when she kisses the welts on my chest do I remember they are there. She kisses each one and then my neck. "You're beautiful, too."

She never fails to break me down.

Any restraint I had flies out the window.

I mold my mouth to hers, gripping her hips and pulling her into me. My chest constricts as she grips my hair and a small moan whispers out of her. I want to take it slow and savor her, but she tastes so good.

"Aryn," she peels her lips away from mine and reaches behind her, her back arching and slivers of her skin pressing against mine and lighting me on fire once again. She turns off the water, although the rain from outside still penetrates through the walls. "We're wasting water. I'm pretty sure all the muds gone, though I don't think I smell very nice." She lifts an arm off my shoulder and sniffs it. "Still smell like soil."

I raise an eyebrow but don't say anything because I'm still breathing heavy, my head fogged over with lust. Instead, I let my body take control and grip the edge of her barely-there tank top. But then I freeze, not wanting to come off too strong. Not wanting to push her.

"Are you going to take it off?" Her eyes are wide, voice shaky. But when her hands come to rest on mine, they are firm and they guide mine upward. After a slow and tortuous ascent, her tank is discarded and her full breasts, snug in of course a blue bra, stare me down.

My pulse beats so loudly in my ears that I can't hear even though I see her mouth moving. She palms my face, a little harder than a caress, a lot softer than a slap.

"What's wrong? Am I... Do you not find me attractive?"

The question catches me off guard, so much so that I can only stare at her. When she tries covering herself, I snap out of it and lean my body against hers, gripping at the skin on her hips. Holding her in place against me.

"Don't cover yourself. Let me see you." I stare into her eyes when I say this because I mean more than her body and I need her to know that. "You drive me crazy with how beautiful you are. And I'm not talking about only your body. It's all of you, inside and out. I'm a mess when it comes to you. You... you make my heart race and my legs shake."

I feel her swallow, her chest heaving against mine, her fingernails digging into my shoulders.

"I don't know what I'm doing... with all this." She motions to our bare skin.

I press my forehead against hers. "That's okay. There's no

rush and I'll never pressure you into doing something you don't want. Okay?"

She nods, a sigh fanning across my face. I slide my hands across her hips, slick, soft skin meeting my palm. She starts to melt, and I become mush under her lips. But then the spell is broken; I feel the scars the same moment she tenses.

She recoils like I've just slapped her and curls herself into the corner of the shower. I can't help but trace the white and soft pink ridges along her hips, marring her sun-kissed skin and reminding me so much of my sister.

"Get out."

I reach for her, but she narrows her eyes at me, although I can tell she's anything but angry. And when she whispers "please," I want to do anything to take the pain out of her voice. But I don't know what to do except leave and wait until she's ready to let me in.

* * *

I pace my room for what feels like an hour before she comes shuffling in, hair tied up in a bun, small frame tightly wrapped in a towel. She has a smaller towel slung across her shoulders, which makes me think she's ready to throw in the towel, quite literally. She closes the door behind her and sighs, before sitting on the floor and leaning against the foot of my bed.

I just stand there and stare as she lets her hair down, wet curls sticking to her skin, framing her face, urging me to bury my fingers in them once again. She brings the towel to her curls and pats them, the towel quickly absorbing the water.

"I had to use your shampoo because I'm pretty sure I had sticks and leaves in my hair." She shrugs, at what I'm not sure.

"It's not tailored for hair like mine, but it'll do." Her voice gets softer and she finally makes eye contact with me. "And I get to smell like you again."

I'm about to combust from all the questions swirling around my head, the lingering lust, and overwhelming concern. I channel it and take a seat next to her, motioning for her to sit between my legs. Surprisingly, she complies and I begin gently drying her hair.

"We have to talk."

She sags against me, defeated. "I know. Just say what you need to."

She flinches when I place my hand against her towel clad hip. "Why would you do this?"

"The cuts were easier to hide there."

Anger flares up in me but I swallow it down. I can't be mad at her. "No, why would you hurt yourself in the first place?"

She huffs and turns to face me, thighs pressing against mine. One hand grips the towel, while the other comes to rest upon my still bare chest. "Same reason these scars are here. The same reason you punch trees." There is a teasing tone to her voice, but her eyes are as serious as I've ever seen them. "It was the only way to control the pain, the darkness. I-I would spend hours curled into a ball crying, days locked in my room."

She gives me a pointed look, like she's saying *you know,* because I do. I just experienced her locking herself in and shutting everyone else out. "But when I cut, I could release some of the hurt. I felt like I could simply bleed it all out. I don't do it anymore, even when I want to. Even when I feel like I desperately need to."

"But you still want to die. You said it in the hallway."

She looks away, muttering, "What does it matter? You said

201

we're dead inside anyway."

I let my anger out now, not because I think people who commit suicide are selfish, but because I fucking love her and if she were to suddenly vanish, if I were to lose her, I don't think I'd be able to recover. I'm still recovering from losing my father. I can't lose her too.

I grip her chin, tight enough so she can't look away. "But you're not dead. You hear me? You're here with me right now, in this moment." I loosen my hold on her, but she leans into me. "I want a million more, no, a lifetime more of moments with you so have to hold on and you have to fight. Even when it gets hard, even when you feel like there are only dark days ahead of you."

Her eyes fill with tears, but they refuse to fall. "I convinced myself that I could go through with it, with ending it all, if I could only make it to graduation. That's why when your mom asked me about college, I couldn't answer. Because I have never allowed myself to think that far ahead."

"Has anything changed?"

She hesitates, biting her lip, which is still red and swollen from me kissing her. Then she slowly shakes her head, "No, I still can't see anything in my future. But..."

Her eyes are closed as if in pain. I lean my forehead against hers. "But what?"

"I don't believe that love can heal all, but ever since I met you, I've wanted to have a future. Even though I can't imagine it, I want you there with me." She wraps her arms around my neck, bringing her shivering form against mine. "I don't want to rely on you, I don't want to put that kind of pressure on you and I can't expect you to fix all my problems. I have to do that, but Aryn, I want to get better if that means I can have you."

She pauses and I know she's not done, but I take the silence as an opportunity to let her words soak in. My entire body is tingly, like someone took a match and lit it along my nerves. My heart beats like I've just had three shots of espresso. As cliché as it sounds, her body fits perfectly against mine and I want nothing more than to love this girl for the rest of my life, to protect her even from herself. My body hums as she continues because she's promising to at least try living. She's letting me in.

"You are a light in the darkness for me, and I'm convinced no one's ever burned as brightly as you do."

We breathe against one another, her words soaking us with all the possibilities of what's to come. I wish I could say more, wish I could coat her in words of assurance, of certainty, of love. But I can tell she's tired of being told what to say, what to do, how to feel. She's tired of words that do nothing to fill the hollow parts of her.

So I lay her down, cover her with my body and warmth, shield her from the darkness she's struggling to fight. I ask her to open herself up to me, to let herself be bare like I have been. I try to be the light she claims I am.

I show her how alive we are.

Learning to Float

Savannah

I missed school for three days and it suddenly turns into a fairytale nightmare. There are pale blue and pink streamers strung in every hallway, like thinly spun cotton candy. Bright, pink flyers are on every hallway corner and on every other locker, jammed into the crevices and shoved into unsuspecting faces.

Everyone seems to be talking in hushed whispers, as if their plans for the very public, school hosted dance are top secret. Even so, their whispers combine and increase in volume until all I can hear are voices eager for eyes; the whole purpose of a secret is for someone to find out what it is.

The shows these people put on are all too much, all too annoying.

I'm grumbling to myself, already in a foul mood after being blinded by all the bright, in-your-face flyers, when Aryn interrupts me.

"Savannah Mitchell." He comes to a standstill in front of me, arms spread wide open and waiting. Even before I touch him,

I can feel his heat and it instantly reminds me of last night. Of the chill in his room, but the warmth of his body. Of the feel of his hands, his fingers, his skin.

I walk into his chest and exhale, letting all my irritation bleed into his cotton shirt.

"I feel like a dick," Aryn suddenly says, squeezing me before grabbing me by the shoulders and pulling me away from his chest. The heat from his body fades.

"Why?"

He rubs the back of his neck, looking around the hallway and motioning to the streamers and fliers. "Well, the dance is tonight and I didn't buy tickets nor did I ask you and yeah, I don't want you to be mad because now "

I put a finger against his lips. "You talk too much when you're nervous." He smiles beneath my finger. "It's fine, really. I didn't want to go to the dance anyway. Not in the mood for cheesy music, grinding, and spiked punch."

He stares at me for a moment, eyes tracing a path from the top of my head to my neck then back up to my lips. "Let me take you somewhere."

I raise an eyebrow, wondering if he's asking to walk me to class. "Where to? Because first period is about to start."

He grins from ear to ear, his depthless eyes never wavering from mine. "Just meet me at your locker during lunch." He takes a step back, sliding his hand down my arm and gripping my fingers. When he lets me go, he winks, "We're playing hooky."

* * *

When the bell rings, my mind can't process what my body is

doing quick enough. My body tingles like every part of me has fallen asleep. I basically sprint through the hallways, bumping shoulders with classmates who are practically strangers. The moment I see him, leaning against my locker like he's done it a thousand times, my heartbeat accelerates.

I quicken my pace and am almost there, just another stretch of hallway, when Clara suddenly appears in front of me. I'm not able to stop in time and we collide, her elbow jutting into my ribcage.

We separate, my breath ragged, and she glares at me.

"Watch where you're going, slut." She smirks, flicking her hair over her shoulder.

My ribs ache, but I roll my eyes at her attempt to be threatening. I'm preparing myself for another verbal attack and clenching my fists in case it gets physical, but Aryn swoops in and wraps his hand around my fist.

"If you don't mind," Aryn begins, uncurling my fingers and sliding his palm over mine. "My girlfriend and I have plans." He starts walking away, me in tow, before he stops and turns back around. He motions to Clara's face. "You have a little bitch, well, everywhere."

Then we're running through the halls, giggling to ourselves, and my heart is back to beating a mile a minute, the word "girlfriend" unfamiliar and exciting. When we reach his car, he presses me against it, like in all the high school romance movies, and kisses me like he's been waiting all day to feel my lips against his. When he pulls away he sucks in a deep breath and ushers me into the car.

"Strap in, Sav." He slides into his seat and rolls down the window, flashing me the smile I see in my dreams, the smile hidden somewhere in my past. "It's adventure time!"

* * *

"So where are you taking me again? Oh right, you won't tell me!" I'm pouting, legs crossed and jumpy in the passenger seat.

"We're almost there, calm down. It's worth the wait, I promise."

"Can I at least have a hint? I'm not very fond of surprises."

Aryn chuckles, reaching his hand out to touch me. A shiver slides through me as his fingers gently press into my knee.

"Look outside," he says, giving my knee a squeeze and leaving me breathless. "My dad used to take me here."

I look out the window and am bombarded by tree after tree, some still bare from winter's harshness and leaning into the path of the sun, hoping the warmth will help them grow. Aryn turns off the main road onto a dirt one and we bounce in our seats, the scenery shaking around us.

"This was our weekend getaway spot." Aryn turns off the ignition and parks the car under the shade of a huge oak tree. He comes around to open my door before I can object, helping me out and then covering my eyes. "Don't peek," he warns, placing a firm hand on the small of my back and pushing me forward.

"Is this the part where you kill me and bury my body parts in the woods?" I stumble on a rock. "Because I've seen the movies; you'll be the number one suspect and will most definitely get caught."

"Shh," he whispers, the rocks crunching underneath our shoes. He suddenly stops and turns me around, planting me firmly in one spot. Then he uncovers my eyes. "Now you can look."

"Oh, wow…" In front of me is a sparkling lake, waves lapping against the bank in a slow, rhythmic motion. There is a slight breeze that smells of pure spring time. I take a deep breath, "This is absolutely gorgeous. I could stay here forever."

Aryn bumps me, causing me to stumble forward. "Well, too bad."

"What?" I shriek as he pushes me forward again, the lapping waves becoming large and luminous under the bright sky. "What are you doing?"

"Today," he flashes a grin at me before shoving me forward again. "You're learning to float."

"Float?" I turn toward him and wrap my arms around his waist, burying my face in his chest.

I feel him nod against me and his chest vibrates. "Yes, on your back. I'm going to teach you."

He pries me off of him and when I gulp, it feels like I swallowed my tongue. I am speechless as he runs back to the car, pulls out two towels from the back seat, and then proceeds to strip in front of me.

"You-you planned this?" My voice is shaky and I clutch my shirt.

"I did," he admits, placing the towels on a smooth rock near the lake's bank. He walks over to me and offers me his hand. "I won't let go of you. I promise." And then he smiles at me and I lose all fight.

"Please don't let me go."

I strip to just my bra and panties and wobble to the edge of the lake, where the water kisses my toes. It's freezing, like those dark, December nights where everything is quiet and still and so cold your body aches.

I start shaking my head, throat closing as images of blue

ribbons flash before my eyes.

"No, no," I whisper, shaking my head more violently now. "Don't make me, Aryn. Please don't make me."

I am suddenly off the ground and in his arms, his bare chest pressed against my barely-clothed one. He wraps my legs around his waist and begins moving toward the water. Before I can protest, he shakes his head.

"You don't want this fear to dictate your whole life." I gulp down whatever tries coming up. "I will never let you go. Do you understand me?"

I'm only able to nod the moment the water touches my foot and I cling to Aryn like the life preserver he is.

The water rises to my waist and I'm shaking so hard it feels like my bones are going to break. I have my eyes squeezed shut, legs clamped around him like a vice. When he loosens his grip, I can only whimper.

"Shh," he tries to soothe. He manages to pry my fingers and legs from around him and repositions me so I'm in his arms bridal style. The water bites my back. "I'm going to lay you back, okay? I'm not letting go. You're doing great."

He holds me against his chest and leans me back, my hair skimming the water. I let my mind go blank, not wanting to be here at this moment. Why would he force me into the water? I'm not ready to confront my fears. I'm not ready to-

He molds his mouth to mine and swallows my cries. He holds me against him until my shivers are absorbed by his skin. I'm crying, but I feel it. The sun, the warmth both from him and the sky.

"I got you. You're okay. You're doing great."

His voice echoes in my head before splitting and becoming three voices. At first, I think I'm going crazy but then I recognize one of the voices. It's my dad, saying "you're okay" over and over again, words slurred like his tongue is frozen. The other voice is slightly deeper, smoother, kinder. I get a snapshot of this man's face, sharp jaw, thin lips, almond eyes; an older version of Aryn.

The image burns bright then turns grainy and the effort of trying to maintain the image makes me groan.

I grip Aryn tighter, "I've been here. This is where it happened."

"Where what happened?"

"Where I drowned. You were there!" I don't mean to scream but the words rip out of me anyway. The pain in my head increases. "Your dad and my dad. We were all there. All here. "

The pain in my head intensifies until I can't feel anything at all.

The Grief of it All

Aryn

No one ever tells you that things fall apart as easily as they come together. That life doesn't grant any favors, doesn't play favorites or give second chances.

Or maybe we're told these things all along and purposely ignore them because we hope that for once, we're the lucky ones.

I don't consider myself lucky at all. Especially not now. Not after I royally screwed up.

It has been four days since Savannah passed out in my arms, shivering like the water seeped right into her bones. I was frantic, everything hazy as I rushed to get her home, to warmth and safety, something I tried so desperately to give her but couldn't. As my mom took care of her, I locked myself away and paced the carpet until it wore thin. I didn't come out until my mom forced me to remember another one of my failures; it's been three years since my dad passed away.

And now, Savannah is home alone like nothing has changed and I'm standing at the gates of the cemetery. All I can think about is the girl who wants to die and the man who is dead and my past has never looked more like my present until now. I'm shaking my head, trying to dislodge images of Savannah drowning and reaching out for me, when my mom places a hand on my shoulder.

"Come on. I think you need a good vent session."

She guides me past the main gates and along the winding path until we reach his headstone, a scrubbed-clean grey block of stone. It reads: David Cooper, 1976 - 2016, loving father, husband, and son.

So generic, so universal. If his name was erased, this headstone could be for anyone. How is it that we live such different lives but in the end, we all look the same? How is it that one sentence or a few etched words can sum up the full lives we live?

My mom runs a hand across the top of the stone, before slowly tracing the letters of his name. After heaving a sigh, she shoots me a weak smile. "I'll be back in a few minutes."

I just stand there, not sure what I want to say, what he would want to hear. After a few moments, my legs give out and I fall to my knees. The ground is damp and the dirt clings to my jeans.

"I wish you were here." It's a whisper, but I know he can hear me. "I feel like I can't ever do anything right and I won't let myself move forward. It's like..." I hiccup on tears I didn't realize were falling. "It's like I'm stuck in the past."

I grip handfuls of the ground and wish I could feel him, just one more time.

"And I'm in love, dad. God," I shake my head and swallow the lump in my throat. "I'm so in love it's ridiculous. I know you're probably wondering what the hell I know about love when I'm only 17, but I know what it looks like because I've seen you and mom. And this *must* be what it feels like."

The wind is soft as it comes rushing around me and it feels good against my warm skin. It wraps around me and gushes through me so that I can continue speaking.

"But I'm such a fuck-up and I can't hold onto anything good. I ruin everything I touch."

The wind comes back full force, angry and purposeful, and I swear I hear his voice. It's faint, like a whisper echoing from the end of a tunnel, but I hear it.

"I miss him."

Corey plops next me, my pulse jumping at his sudden appearance. But I guess I knew he'd show up sooner or later. He always does.

"Life without him is so bland, you know? Like a whole array of colors have been erased from the world."

I can only nod and lean into him as he speaks, knowing he'll hold me up.

"When I think of him, I think of pillow forts and warm sand between our toes. I think of learning to shave, how to change a tire, how to be brave."

"He taught us a lot, didn't he?" He could have taught us more, could have taught my children things I'd never learn to do properly.

"He did live a full life, you know?"

"But it was cut short. Because of me." I have no energy to raise my voice or shed any more tears. I feel drained.

"He never blamed you."

Both Corey and I look up at my mom, dressed in all black like it's a funeral. And maybe it is. Maybe every time she comes here it's like burying him all over again.

"What happened was tragic, but I try to believe that it was his time to go." She collapses onto the ground and folds into herself. "It's never going to be fair." She wraps her arms around both of us, trying to hold all of our pain in. "And it'll hurt for a long time, maybe forever. But we'll survive, for each other and for him. That's what he would want." She smiles through her tears.

There is a beat of silence, a hush that soothes as much as it stings.

"Did you tell him about Savannah?" Corey breaks up the hurt with a waggle of his eyebrows. My mom lets loose a laugh and nudges me.

"Your dad absolutely loved her. She was always over, she was a part of our family."

Corey purses his lips. "It's still so strange you don't remember being friends when you were kids."

My mom shakes her head. "Not really," she says. "Not only were you both so young, but it truly was traumatic." Her breath stutters. "And Savannah's parents blamed your dad for the accident."

"Wait, wait, what?" Corey asks my question before I get the chance. But he doesn't capture the amount of disbelief I have.

"I-I don't know exactly what happened, but they blamed your dad and after that, Savannah never came over anymore. You asked about her all the time, but as the months went by, you asked less and less until you stopped asking altogether. It seemed like it was easier to deal with the loss if you forgot and that's what you did."

"But why would they blame dad? He would never hurt Savannah."

She nods, "I feel like they had to blame anyone else other

than themselves in order to cope. But it didn't change anything. Even before the lake or Savannah's depression, her parents weren't ever really there. She was an accident they couldn't get rid of and they never tried hiding it."

My chest hurts for multiple reasons. "And after the accident...?"

"They used her trauma as an excuse to not be parents. I know it doesn't make sense, but that's what happened."

"It's fucked up is what it is." Corey's words hang in the air as we process the past.

As we sit there, letting the past blend in with the present, we grieve, we laugh, and my god, do we hurt. But when we get up to go, the tightness in my chest loosens. Not completely because that's not how grieving or healing works. But it's a start.

Coming to Terms

Savannah

My body is once again cemented over. My limbs feel so disconnected that when I try to move, nothing happens. I thought I'd be in pain, but the shock of the water wasn't nearly as physically damaging as it was mentally. I'm not even upset with Aryn because after all, he didn't truly force me into the water. But what rocked me straight to the core was all the memories that became dislodged. It was like being in the place where it all started caused the memories to slip back into focus. Some will be lost forever, others are still just colors and sounds, but a select few are so clear it's like watching a movie.

I've been hiding in my room for the past few days, trying to stitch these memories together in chronological order. Even now, I close my eyes so I can concentrate on the past I never knew I had. But I hear the door slam, the sound shaking the empty bones of this house and it rattles me, too. This house has been mine and mine alone for so long that an uninvited presence seems intrusive, cruel.

I tiptoe out of my room and pause right outside the door,

waiting to hear creaks or groans. When I hear shuffling coming from my parent's room, I sneak to their bedroom door and peek inside.

Standing there, like an apparition on the verge of disappearing, is my dad. He has a suitcase laid open on the carpeted floor and is throwing handfuls of clothes into it. I push the door open wider.

"Are we moving?"

He jumps, turning around to face me. "Jesus, you scared me. Don't do that."

"Did you and mom decide to sell the house? Should I start packing?"

He raises an eyebrow. "What do you mean? Your mom isn't selling the house."

"Then why are you packing your clothes?"

He sighs, as if my questions are exhausting him. "Didn't your mother tell you?"

I know I shouldn't ask because deep down, I know this won't end well. "Tell me what?"

"Savannah," his voice and my name do not make a good combination. The way he says my name reminds me of a tin can scraping across concrete. "Your mom and I are divorced. We've been divorced for over a year now. We just didn't know the right time to tell you and now, well, I'm coming to finally collect my things."

I take a deep breath but it gets stuck in my chest. Everything inside me tightens until my entire body feels like a rubber band about to snap. "I-I don't understand..."

"I'm not sure why your mother would lie to you. She's only making the situation worse."

The rubber band gets pulled tighter. "But then... Where

have you been this whole time? Why couldn't you have still called me or visited me?"

"I didn't have time."

"You had no time?"

"Listen, I don't have to explain this all to you."

I take a step toward him, fingers digging into my palm. "Yes the hell you do."

His eyes barrel into me. "Don't you dare speak to me like that."

"Then explain to me why you didn't have time."

"I met someone, okay?" He pulls out more clothes from the dresser and dumps them into the suitcase, which is suddenly almost full. "I met someone and we picked up where we both left off. She has two teenage daughters, just like you. I had to spend all my time making that family work."

"But you couldn't make this one work?" The rubber band snaps and is replaced by a ticking time bomb. "I needed you." I hate how pathetic I sound, like I'm a child being chastised.

"I couldn't be here for you. It was too much."

"What was too much?"

He jabs a finger against his skull. "Whatever you had going on in here. Your mother and all the doctors said it was a disease but I just don't believe that. I never did."

"What do you think it is then?"

"It's nothing!" He snaps his suitcase shut and zips it up. "You just need to toughen up, kid. Life isn't kind to the weak." He walks past me, suitcase dangling from his fingers. I follow after him, barely able to keep up as he rushes down the stairs.

"I'm sick, dad. Not weak. The doctors said-"

"Just excuses." He drops the suitcase by the front door, where the boxes Jacklyn, Abby, and I packed up all those weeks ago sit. The ticking in my chest gets louder, faster.

"So that's it? I was too much to handle and so you pick up and leave and start a whole new family?"

"It's not that simple."

"Bullshit. You can't just decide to leave and forget about us just because it's too difficult. That's not how life works!"

He shrugs and decides I'm not even worth the words. As he heads into the kitchen and opens the cupboard housing his favorite mug, I panic.

"You were there when I drowned."

This makes him pause, hand midair. He sighs again and closes the cupboard, turning to face me. When he leans against the counter, it feels like a threat, a challenge. "We all were. But it was David's fault."

I shake my head. "No, it wasn't. I remember. You were watching me and you were drinking-"

"You don't know what you're talking about."

"Yes," I'm speaking fast now, my thoughts and memories tumbling out of my mouth in a frantic effort to stay vivid. "You were drinking and you let me go into the water. You..." My head hurts again, the images becoming fuzzy. "You fell asleep and I was calling for help and you didn't come. You didn't come save me!"

"You don't remember anything." He attempts to come toward me but I back away. "The doctors said oxygen deprivation can permanently erase memories."

I'm shaking my head and trembling and fighting to stay on my feet. "No, no. I remember that day." I meet his gaze and lower my voice. "I remember everything you did to me."

He pauses again, eyes narrowing. Then without a word, he backtracks to the cupboard and takes his mug off the shelf. My head swirls and I want to hit him and I want to cry, but I still don't want him to leave. If he leaves, he is taking a part of me with him. Everything he has packed and wants to take out of this house is a thread in all that I am. If the house is emptied, so am I .

"You don't have to leave. I want you to stay."

He sighs again, and this time a bomb does go off inside me. I can barely breathe as he looks me dead in the eye and delivers the last punch I can take: "I can't. I don't want to." I can only listen as he stomps back up the stairs, leaving me to deal with my own debris.

I stumble to the kitchen table, my skin feeling like it's peeling away from the bone. I want to squeeze myself so tightly that I burst. Everything hurts.

Everything hurts.

And I want to grab the nearest knife or I want to bash my head against the kitchen sink. I want to see red because then maybe everything will feel okay. Maybe then everything will make sense.

Instead I set my palms under the kitchen table and lift. It flips over, the loud crash echoing against the still empty house, even though there is more than just my corpse here now. But it doesn't help. And it doesn't stop all their words from filling me up.

Make sure you eat.

Did you take your medicine?

You never want to do anything.

Do you even smile?

Just be a good girl.

I have new daughters.

You're sick.

You're replaceable.
You're not good enough.
You're not good enough!
I AM NOT GOOD ENOUGH!

Before I even realize it, I'm tearing through the front door, snatching my father's keys on the way out. If he wants to leave so badly, I'm going to make him work for it.

I slide into the driver's seat and then pause. How many times have I driven? Am I stable enough to drive? If I crash, will this be how I die? Trapped by metal and suffocating from the impact of a tree?

I take a shaky breath, start the car, and slowly peel out of the driveway. Once my body stops shaking, I roll down the windows and slam my foot against the gas pedal. I need to feel the wind against my face, the cool sting of the spring weather. I hiccup against the tears threatening to leave me, against the knot forming in my throat. I just need to get there, to be at the edge of everything.

I need to let go.

The Truth

Aryn

I've always been able to tell when someone is on the brink of imploding. I see in myself every time I look in the mirror. I've seen it in strangers' faces when we pass by one another on the street. I see it every time I look at Savannah, feel it every time I touch her. Yet I never actually thought about what happens *after* a person implodes. How do we pick up their scattered pieces? How do we cope knowing we saw all the signs yet couldn't prevent their undoing?

These are the questions I'm trying to answer when Corey gets the call from Jacklyn.

The minute he picks up, I hear screaming. He glances at me, eyes wide, but holds fast to the phone against his ear. I know from the volume of the conversation and Corey's position, perched on the very edge of the couch, that something is wrong.

The call is short, but seems to last an eternity as I wait for Corey to break the news to me. Finally, he pockets his phone and heaves me off the couch. When I'm standing, he keeps his hands firmly on my shoulders, holding me in place.

"Savannah's gone."

I'm glad he's holding me because my legs can't seem to support me any longer.

5 minutes later, we're in my mom's car and she's driving us around the woods to Savannah's house because I'm numb and my legs can't carry me fast enough. The door is wide open when we pull up and there is dirt upturned all over the driveway.

There are boxes, a mug, and a suitcase neatly lined up by the front door. With Savannah gone, I expected a cold emptiness and quiet. Her parents may pay for it, but this is her house and without her here, it should be in shambles. But there *is* chaos everywhere, in the voices fighting for dominance in the kitchen and echoing off the walls, and in the slumped shoulders of Savannah's closest friends.

I see Bailey first, mascara running streaks down her cheeks. Her body is trembling like mine and I wish we had the strength to support one another. She turns to me, a silent plea in her eyes, and whispers, "She's going to do it. I can feel it."

I want to reassure her, contradict her, but there are other eyes in the kitchen. Eyes that scream, eyes that are wet, eyes that are unfocused and jumping from person to person.

The chaos is worse here. The kitchen table is turned over, everything that sat on it scattered across the floor. But the most chaotic thing in this house, aside from Savannah not being here, is the man casually leaning against the counter, whiskey bottle in hand. There is a war here and he's the one who started it.

I step further into the room and when he finally looks at me, it's like he's seen a ghost. Immediately, I know he's seeing

223

my father in my cheekbones, in my mouth, in my shoulders. I open my mouth, eager to say something, but not sure what, but Bailey must've been tired of the ceasefire because she speaks first.

"Where is she? What did you say to her?" Bailey yells until her face is red and takes a step toward Savannah's father like she wants to hit him. I won't be the one to stop her.

He looks at my mom and smirks. "What is up with teenagers thinking they can disrespect adults?"

My mom, who has been standing in the kitchen's doorway, comes further into the room and stands by the upside down table. She is the only division between us and him.

"Marcus," my mom sighs, looking around the room. "What the hell happened?"

Marcus shrugs, extending the whiskey bottle to her, which she shakes her head at. "Beats me. She over exaggerated like usual."

"Oh you drunk piece of shit!" Jacklyn, who is always the most composed one, tries storming past my mother, who merely wraps her arms around Jacklyn and holds her in place. "I swear to God, if she hurts herself I'll kill you."

Marcus purses his lips, liquid hanging off the miniscule hair framing his mouth and chin. "Jia," my mom flinches when he says her name. "Tell these children to get out of grown folks' business."

Again, she sighs. "Just tell us what happened, Marcus."

"We want the truth!" Bailey interrupts, face red. "No more lies. You and Sarah have done nothing but lie to her and now we want the truth."

"The truth," he exhales and licks his lips. "Is that I came to this house and did what I always do. I hurt her."

I manage to evade my mother's hands as I walk up to Marcus and grip his shirt. He's taller than me by quite a few inches, but he's barely able to hold himself upright because of the alcohol. "What the fuck did you do?"

Although drunk off his ass, he still manages to push me and I stumble into one of the table's upright legs.

Mom comes in between us, holding her hands out. "If you touch my son one more time, Marcus, you'll be in the hospital for more than just alcohol poisoning." Then she turns to me. "Let's all take a deep breath."

"Yeah," Marcus jeers. "This doesn't concern you, Aryn."

"Of course it does. She's my girlfriend. I know more about her-"

"You don't know anything! You're just a kid."

"Please," pleads Bailey, coming to stand beside me. "Just tell us what happened. We need to find her."

"I was a drunk piece of shit." He lifts the bottle of whiskey in Jacklyn's direction. "Still am."

My mom lifts her now trembling hands to her mouth. "What did you do to her, Marcus?"

"I just told her everything her mother wouldn't: that we're no longer together, that I have a new family, that I couldn't be *here,* not when everything was always about her wanting to die." There is spit flying out of his mouth. "She is so weak." He pushes himself off of the counter.

All of us immediately shift, preparing to let fists fly if need be. But he's not done talking and we have to listen.

"You know, I used to get so angry. She was either always crying or just... numb." He reaches both arms out like she is in front of him. "I would just shake her, hoping she would snap out of it." The whiskey swishes inside the bottle as he rapidly moves his hands.

"She was just a little girl." This is Abby, who until now has been silently huddled in the corner, huge teardrops cascading down her cheeks. Now she grips at the skin near her collarbone like she can feel his hands on her.

"I never wanted her," he admits, licking his lips. "Sometimes I would look at her and wish she would just disappear." He brings the bottle to his lips, but hesitates. His eyes are bloodshot, shiny. "I locked her in a closet once. By the time I remembered, it had been hours. When I finally opened the door," he shakes his head. "She was just sitting there, like a doll. Still." He takes a long, harsh tug on the bottle. "After that she would mention the darkness all the time. Like those few hours in the closet let it inside her."

My mom walks up to him and rips the bottle from his grasp, throwing it to the floor and sending pieces of glittering glass everywhere. "You abused her, Marcus! And you have the audacity to feel sorry for yourself?" I expect her to slap him, but she makes a fist and delivers it across his jaw. "She's better off without you."

He tries defending himself, cradling his jaw and holding up one finger. "I hit her once but that was all it took. Sarah noticed the bruise and kicked me out. But she's no saint herself. She leaves the girl here all the time and there's nothing but white walls and echoes here." He motions to the overturned kitchen, a disarray of broken glass and out of place furniture. "At least I have the decency to stay away. Sarah continues to torture Savannah with the idea of having a family."

Bailey's face has gone completely red. "She has a family. It just doesn't include you."

He shrugs and goes to lift his hand before he remembers the

whiskey is now spreading across the floor. He looks around the room, at each of us and then at the overturned table. "Look at this mess…"

My mom nurses her knuckles and it looks like she may swing again. "It's a mess you made."

Abby wipes at her face. "Where do you think she went?" She's asking us, but Marcus answers anyway.

"She's probably with that damn weed."

"The tulip?"

"Yeah," he waves his hand through the air. "We planted that together a little after the accident. But she's always been obsessed with it."

"Probably because you left right after and that's the only good memory she has of you!" Bailey seethes.

Again, he shrugs. "You were there, too." He looks at me now. "You helped plant it. Look over there." He points to an open notebook on the ground near the fridge, white pages filled with sprawling black ink.

"That's Savannah's journal." Bailey comments, picking it up and flipping through a few pages. Finally, she stops at one and gives it to me.

When I see the picture there, I'm able to finally put all the pieces together. I am in the picture, hands in the dirt around her precious flower, standing by her side. There is another picture of us holding hands and I am smiling wider than I ever thought possible. I nod to myself, realizing that Savannah and I have always been in each other's lives. We just got lost for a while.

"I read some of that." Marcus walks over the broken glass. "You should run while you can. She's truly messed up." He points at his head.

"I love her."

It's enough reason for me, but he obviously doesn't agree.

"Love isn't always enough."

My mom places her hands, so gentle like I might just break, on my shoulders. "There's nothing here for us right now. Let's go."

She steers all of us toward the door, leaving Marcus to deal with the aftermath of his actions.

When we get to the door, I pause and think of the picture on her wall where she's standing at the edge of the world.

I suck in a breath. "I think I know where she is."

I just hope we're not too late.

Free Falling

Savannah

I am at the edge of everything.

The wind is strong up here, pushing me back from the ledge every time I draw near. My skin tingles and when I press my fingers into my forearms, it stings. In fact, my entire body is the type of numb that sends painful jolts to every nerve and muscle.

I've never felt more alive than I do balancing here, so close to the end. As I look down at the waves crashing against the rocky cliff, I don't wish to be there, body broken beyond repair or recognition. But I also don't wish to be back there, where I am questioned, quarantined, pitied. If I could stay here, in this sort of in-betweenness, this almost nothingness, then I would be content.

But how can I be content when no one lets me be? When no one lets me simply disappear and cease to exist?

"Savannah!"

There is the voice I've come to love and yearn for. But when I turn away from the waves and face him, his presence makes my skin itch. Surely, he won't ruin this for me will he?

From behind him comes my friends, my caregivers, my kryptonite. Because if not for them, I would have been gone long ago. But I held on for them, for me, for us. Maybe I shouldn't have.

My head spins before they even speak, but when they do, the wind stalls. Is it quiet so it can laugh at their pleas, their ultimatums? Or does it yearn, like me, for something or someone to bring it back, to bring it peace?

"Savannah, sweetie, step back from the ledge, okay?" Jacklyn stands next to Jia, upholding her position as mom of the group. Their facial expressions are so similar, worry lines around their mouth, furrowed brows, that I don't know which one of them spoke.

I just shake my head. "I don't think I can."

"Why not?"

"There's nothing here for me anymore. Nothing *there*."

Abby steps up to the plate now, mouth downturned and eyes baggy. "We're here. Are we not worth you sticking around?"

I hold myself around the waist. "I lasted far longer than I thought I could."

Bailey walks toward me, ten steps closer than I should allow, close enough that I imagine I can feel the heat from her skin.

"Do you remember," she starts, a smile trying to pull up her lips. "When we started high school and we were just scrawny, pimpled girls who didn't know up from down?"

I do. I remember that year because it was easy to be invisible, easier to lose myself when I was still becoming someone.

"We made a promise to graduate together and apply to the same colleges. We said we'd never let anyone, especially our parents, stomp on what our future could be." She holds my gaze for a moment. "So why are you letting your dad get in the way?"

"You don't understand." I plead, but I'm not sure for what. "My entire life he's never wanted me, never wanted to touch me. Never hugged me. Like I was a disease, like I was dirty." The wind rustles from behind me and I close my eyes. "And now that I can remember what he's done to me, it seems like I'm just meant to be hurt. To hurt."

"He's never been a father and he took his own insecurities out on you. But that doesn't mean you deserved any of it. Do you hear me?"

I nod, hearing her but not believing her.

"Should I want to dic? Was I just born broken?" I'm asking all of them, because if I am broken, does that mean I can be fixed? I open my eyes and notice that they've all come closer, Bailey and Aryn just a few feet from me. I instinctively take a step back and feel rocks shift beneath me.

"No! No, Sav, you're not broken." Aryn holds his hands out to me, like he always does, showing me he means no harm, that he's making room for me. "Sometimes people just feel so much that it's overwhelming. That it hurts and it takes and it is relentless. That's how you feel, right?"

"Yes, all the time. Everything or nothing." He takes a step forward and I want him to hold me so badly that I nearly take off running. "But am I the only one? Does that make me a freak?"

"No, not at all." Jacklyn is shivering, but stands tall. "I feel like that sometimes, too and I go to counseling once a month to talk about it."

I stare at her, following the movement of her lips as she talks. "But... you never said anything."

She sends me a sad smile, "You never asked."

A sharp pain pierces my gut and then my chest. I take a shuddering breath, hoping to ease the pain, but it only spreads to my head. Have I been so self-obsessed that I never noticed the suffering of others? Am I the one who doesn't listen, who speaks over those who hide their hurt?

"No, no." I cry out, hands coming up to cover my ears as the wind comes back full force. It pushes and pulls and whispers for me to ride it so that I don't have to feel the pain anymore. I take another step back.

"Savannah!" Aryn calls out for me again. I lock eyes with him and swim in the tears forming and falling from them. "I need you to hold on, okay? I need you to fight." He's repeating words from that night, making me remember the feel of his skin and the warmth of his promises. "I'm the light, right?" I nod, hand reaching out for him before I can stop it. "You're the light for me. You make everyday brighter. I can't live without it, without you."

He keeps going, words moving faster than his legs. "We love you. *I* love you, Savannah. And we have so many new memories to make, remember? We still have to visit China and you have to teach me how to edit photos and you still need to learn how to float on your back." I just keep nodding. "Please don't do this. You don't have to do this. You don't have to be scared anymore."

I stop reaching for him and shake my head. "I'm not scared. I'm just so tired."

I want to feel the wind work to support me.

It must feel so good to be weightless, to be nothing.

But I want to feel him as badly as I want to feel nothing.

I can only watch as Aryn takes miniscule steps toward me.

My body wants to recoil, but my mind and my heart yearns for him. To feel the warmth in his fingertips. To have him tell me it'll all be okay, even if it's a lie. He reaches out to me and again, I do the same, taking a step away from the ledge, away from the freefall.

Rocks crumble and I see the sky and it's all so bright. Just like him. The light in the darkness for me. I feel his arms the same moment I hear the wind rush around me. I have to close my eyes because I don't want to see what's happening. Even if I wanted it, I can't stomach seeing the waves reach out for me. But I can't handle seeing their eyes on me, either. I don't want to see, but I can feel it.

I'm finally free.

About the Author

Deasia Hawkins - pen name D.J. Hawkins - is an upstate NY native. She holds a BA in Literature and a Masters of Teaching in English Education. In addition to writing, she also teaches special education to middle school students.

Besides English, Deasia speaks German and is trying her best to learn Spanish and American Sign Language. She currently lives in southern Massachusetts with her cat Tofu.

Be on the lookout for her novel "Quietus," an adult dark fantasy romance, and her poetry book "Faultlines" coming in 2021!

You can connect with me on:
- https://www.thedjhawkins.com
- https://twitter.com/deasia_hawkins
- https://www.facebook.com/DJ-Hawkins-103843541484680
- https://www.instagram.com/d.j.hawkins